D0199567

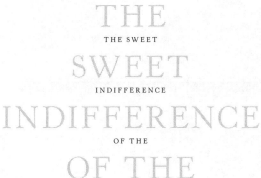

THE SWEET

INDIFFERENCE

OF THE

WORLD

PETER STAMM

Translated from the German by Michael Hofmann

OTHER PRESS / NEW YORK

We wish to express our appreciation to the Swiss Arts Council Pro Helvetia
for their assistance in the preparation of this translation.

Production editor: Yvonne E. Cárdenas
Text designer: Jennifer Daddio / Bookmark Design & Media Inc.
This book was set in Horley Old Style MT by
Alpha Design & Composition of Pittsfield, NH

1 3 5 7 9 10 8 6 4 2

Library of Congress Cataloging-in-Publication Data

Names: Stamm, Peter, 1963- author. | Hofmann, Michael, 1957 August 25-
translator.
Title: The sweet indifference of the world / Peter Stamm ; translated from
the German by Michael Hofmann.
Other titles: Sanfte Gleichgültigkeit der Welt. English
Description: New York : Other Press, [2020] | "Originally published in
German as Die sanfte Gleichgültigkeit der Welt in 2018
by S. Fischer Verlag GmbH, Frankfurt am Main."
Identifiers: LCCN 2019005601 (print) | LCCN 2019011396 (ebook) |
ISBN 9781590519806 (ebook) | ISBN 9781590519790 (paperback)
Subjects: LCSH: Young women—Fiction. | Older men—Fiction. |
Fate and fatalism—Fiction. | Memory—Fiction.
Classification: LCC PT2681.T3234 (ebook) | LCC PT2681.T3234 S2613 2020 (print)
| DDC 833/.92—dc23
LC record available at https://lccn.loc.gov/2019005601

"We lay there without moving.
But under us all moved, and moved us,
gently, up and down, and from side to side."

—SAMUEL BECKETT, *Krapp's Last Tape*

THE SWEET INDIFFERENCE OF THE WORLD

ONE

She visits me often, usually at night. She stands by my bed, looking down at me, and says, You've aged. She doesn't say it in a nasty way, though, her voice sounds affectionate, almost merry. She sits down on the side of the bed. But then your hair, she says, tousling it with her hand, it's as thick as it ever was. Only it's gone white. You're not getting any older though, I say to her. I'm not sure if that's a happy thought for me or not. We never talk much, after all, what is there to say. The time goes by. We look at each other and smile.

She comes almost every night, sometimes so late that it's starting to get light. She was never one for punctuality, but I don't mind about that, the less time I have left, the more time I allow myself. I don't do anything but wait anyway, and the later she comes, the more time I have to look forward to her.

This morning I woke up early and got up right away. For once I didn't want to be in bed when she came. I put on my good pair of pants, my jacket, and the black shoes, and sat down at the table in front of the window. I want to be ready.

It's been cold for days, there's been snow lying on the roofs and fields, and thin lines of smoke twisting up out of the village chimneys. I take the little passe-partout frame with Magdalena's photo out of my desk drawer, it's the picture I clipped from the newspaper ages ago, and you can hardly make her out on it. The paper is yellowed, but it's the only picture of her I have, and barely a day passes that I don't at least glance at it. I run my fingers along the narrow frame and it gives me the feeling I'm touching her, her skin, her hair, her body.

When I look up again, out of the window, I can see her standing outside. Her breath is steaming, and she's smiling and waving. Her lips are moving, and I'm guessing she's calling me. Come on! she repeats, so exaggeratedly that I can lip-read it. Let's go for a walk. I'm coming, I call back, wait for me! My wheezing alarms me, it's an old man's voice, a voice that's just as alien to me as the frail body that imprisons me. I pull on my coat and scarf as quickly as I can. I hurry downstairs, stumbling on the hollowed-out stone steps. By the time I'm walking out of the home, I see Magdalena has already set out. I set off after her, in the direction of the river, toward the footbridge that leads across to the village I grew up in, passing the little pond where we used to feed the ducks when we were little, the place I had a bad fall on my bike, and that other place we used to meet at when we were teenagers at night, and light bonfires. It feels to me as though I've become part of the scenery here, which has hardly changed over all the years.

Magdalena has almost reached the bridge. Her step is so light, it's as though she's levitating over the snowy footpath. In my haste I've forgotten my cane, and I'm torn between my fear of slipping on the ice and falling and my other fear of losing Magdalena from view. Wait! I repeat, I'm not so fast anymore.

Images surface of her vanishing into the mountains before me, how we wandered around the city together, how we traipsed through Stockholm arm in arm, that night I told her my story, and hers, the night she kissed me. She turns to face me and smiles. Come on! she cries. Come and get me.

TWO

TWO

Magdalena must have been perplexed by my message. I hadn't left any number or address, only a time and a place and my first name: Please come to Skogskyrkogården tomorrow at two. I have a story I want to tell you.

I waited for her at the exit to the Underground station. Quarter past two, and she still wasn't there; briefly I thought she might have taken a cab. But her lateness wasn't significant, she was always unpunctual, not in the aggressive way of showing the person waiting that their time is worth less than hers, more from a kind of vagueness with which she approached everything in her life. I was certain that she would come, that her curiosity was greater than her suspicion.

Five minutes later, the next train rolled in, and I was already thinking she wasn't in this one either when she came down the steps with her twinkling feet. I had meant to indicate my presence immediately, but in the instant I saw her, I couldn't breathe, no more than I had been able to the night before when I had stood outside her hotel waiting, and hadn't managed to speak to her then. She must be almost thirty, fully twenty years younger than me, but her manner was that of a girl, and anyone seeing us together would surely suppose we were father and daughter. I let her walk past without addressing her, and then I followed her in the direction of the cemetery.

She didn't make the impression of someone with an appointment to keep, walking down the street with rapid steps, as though she'd been that way a hundred times. I had expected her to stop at the entrance to the cemetery, but she walked straight in, and without the least hesitation climbed the hill that was surmounted by a ring of old trees. At the foot of the hill was an enormous stone cross, and yet the whole site had a heathen aspect, landscape and nature seemed stronger than the consecrated buildings and their Christian symbolism.

Magdalena had sat down at the foot of one of the bare trees up on the hill, and was looking in my direction, as though we were having a race and she'd won. Out of breath, I came level with her, and although she had never seen me before, she seemed to understand straightaway that it was I who had summoned her. Lena, she said, holding out her hand. Christoph, I said, and shook it, in some perplexity. Not Magdalena, then? No one calls me that, she said with a smile. A slightly unusual place for a meeting. I just wanted us to be able to talk undisturbed, I said.

I sat down next to her, and we gazed down at the yellow stone buildings that were probably from the Thirties. Next to a few slabbed structures was a monumental roof supported by square pillars, with a large, frozen pond in front of it. The gently contoured lawn was flecked with snow. From the entrance to the cemetery came people in dark coats, some alone, others in pairs or small groups. They stopped in front of one of the buildings, a scattered group that didn't seem to cohere properly.

I like cemeteries, said Lena. I know, I replied. It's cold, she said, shall we walk a bit?

We walked down the hill. The mourners by now had vanished under the jutting roof of the chapel, and the plaza was once more unoccupied. Next to the building stood a candelabra with a clock. Curious, said Lena, doesn't it look like something on a railway platform? She stood under the clock, looked up at it, checked her watch like a traveler impatient for a train to leave. Final destination, I said. She laughed at me, but carried on playing her role, till I clapped gently, whereupon she gave a clumsy bow.

We walked on into the cemetery, past geometrical rows of graves towards a thin copse of firs. We were walking side by side, so close that sometimes our shoulders brushed. Lena was silent now, but it wasn't an impatient silence, and we could have gone on like that for a long way without talking, just preoccupied with our own thoughts. Finally, just as we stepped between the first trees, I stopped and said, I'd like to tell you my story. She didn't reply but turned towards me and gave me a look that wasn't so much curious as utterly open.

I am a writer, I said, or rather I used to be a writer. I published a book fifteen years ago. My boyfriend's a writer, she said, or hopes to be. I know, I said, that's why I want to tell you my story.

We walked slowly along the gravel path that led in a straight line through the wood, and I told Lena of the strange encounter fourteen years before which had led to my abandoning writing.

THREE

THREE

It was when I was at university that I had first started working on fiction, ambitious projects full of deep wisdom and literary allusions, that no one wanted to read, much less publish. It was these years of trying and failing that finally brought me success. The hero of the novel with which I eventually found a publisher was, just as I was, a disillusioned author. The book was a love story, it was supposed to be a portrait of my girlfriend, but while I was writing it, we broke up, and so it turned into an account of our breakup and the impossibility of love. For the first time in my writing, I had the feeling I was creating a living world. At the same time, I could feel reality slipping through my fingers, daily life was getting boring and shallow to me. Yes, my girlfriend left me, but if I am to be honest I had left her months before in my imagination, I had slipped into fiction and my artificial world. When she told me she couldn't go on this way, and that she was missing me even when I was right there next to her, all I felt was a sense of irritation and exasperation.

My novel, though, was a hit with booksellers and readers; even the reviewers seemed to sit up. This debut promised all sorts of things for the future, wrote one woman. And in fact I did believe in some sort of future, for the first time in a while. After living from hand to mouth for several years, the success of my book secured not a lavish but a respectable income; but above all I had something to show for myself that justified all my endeavors. The years of failed writing already felt like a long-distant time, in which I was caught up in labyrinthine plots, and driven by exaggerated ambitions.

I never admitted how much my story was about me. When I was asked about that after readings, I dismissed the idea, and insisted on the separation between author and narrator.

My publisher had lined up a series of readings for me, and I enjoyed being able to escape my empty apartment and travel around the country, looking at new places, and just being busy for an hour or two in the evenings. When I got an invitation from the little bookshop in my native village, I only briefly hesitated. The old bookseller had written me such a gracious and flattering letter that I agreed. Only as the date moved ever nearer, I felt a little uneasy about reading in front of people who had known me as a boy, and who couldn't fail to make the connection between the characters in my novel and me in my present life.

It was the end of November. I had set off, deliberately early, just after lunchtime. I hadn't been back to the village for years, and I wanted to see if the reality still corresponded with my memory.

The train emptied as it went along, as though approaching a forbidden zone, I was the only person left in my carriage, and it was a long time since the conductor had last put in an appearance. When I set out, the sun was shining, but the farther east we went, the foggier it got, and by now everything outside was gray, forest, bare trees, fallow fields, a herd of sheep, and just the occasional farm or clump of houses. Shortly before the destination, the otherwise straight rail tracks curved hard to cross to the opposite side of the river. Just before the curve, the train slowed down and came to a complete halt. The tilt of the carriage, which had been barely discernible as we were moving, now that we were stopped made me feel giddy, it was as though I was off kilter myself. The train remained standing for a long time, then it gave a jerk and trundled across the river, without anything having happened that would explain the delay. But my sense of unease persisted until I was in the village.

In winter, the region was often fogbound for weeks on end, and those were the climatic conditions I associated with my childhood, a cold, gray, blotting-paper world, but simultaneously cloistered, in which things that weren't directly in front of you seemed not to exist. Only when I took my final school exams and left the village for the city did I learn how large and uncertain the world truly was. Perhaps that was what had prompted me to start writing, to reclaim the landscape and the security of my childhood, from which I had exiled myself.

Although I could perfectly well have gone home when my reading was over, I had asked the bookseller to reserve a room for me in the hotel on the marketplace, which housed a restaurant and a small studio theater as well. Before I went away to college, I had spent a couple of months there, working as a night porter. At that time, the little arts center was still pretty new, and it all seemed very big and terribly modern to me; now it looked modest, old, and run-down.

I had meant to go for a little stroll through the village, but even on the way from the station to the hotel I had been piqued and upset by the mixture of new and familiar. Even those buildings that still looked the way I remembered them seemed strange to me, as though they were in a museum, detached from their context and function.

The air in the hotel room was dry and scented with air freshener. I lay down on the bed and thought about the village the way it used to be. When I shut my eyes, everything was still as it was, the buildings, the streets, the people who lived in them. I remembered the bustle of market days, the processions and celebrations with brass bands and fireworks, but also dim days of spring, the yawning void of summer, the cozy feeling of rainy days in autumn. Each season had had its particular smell, rain on asphalt, hot tar, moldering leaves. Even the snow had had a smell, a kind of dimmed freshness that I could almost taste.

I heard a chiming and woke up. It was dark in the room, and it took me a while to locate the telephone and reply. It was the bookseller, calling to check that I'd arrived and whether he should pick me up at the hotel. I can find my own way, I said, I haven't been away that long.

My previous anxieties turned out to have been misplaced. I didn't know anyone in the audience, and no one seemed to be interested in the fact that I had grown up in their village. After the reading, there were the standard questions, the listeners seemed to have no interest in anything personal. Later I went along with the bookseller and one or two of his customers for a glass of wine in a restaurant. Even though we didn't have much to say to each other, time passed and it got late. I asked after a few people in the village, but most of them were either unknown to the present company or known just by name, having moved away or grown old and no one minding about them anymore. Instead, they talked about all sorts of village subjects, political intrigues, bits of tittle-tattle about people I didn't know and had nothing to do with. When the bar closed at midnight, I had trouble keeping the bookseller from walking me back to the hotel.

During the short walk through the dark and empty streets, for the first time that day, I felt a kind of familiarity, but it was less a matter of the place than the time of night, which evoked memories of going home at the end of pub crawls, endless goodbyes with friends at crossroads, before we each went our separate ways, all our lofty plans and great expectations.

The hotel entrance was down a dimly lit arcade, the glass door was locked. I pushed the after-hours bell. As I was waiting I noticed I was completely drunk. I pressed one hand against the cold glass. After a while, I rang the bell a second time. I remembered doing my rounds when I used to be night porter there. With flashlight in hand I had walked through the theater, across the empty stage, through empty passageways and conference rooms, and down to the underground car park.

Finally, I heard a door bang, and shortly afterwards saw movement in the corridor, the inner glass door opened, and a young man approached me. While he fiddled around with the lock, I saw his face next to the reflection of my own, but not until he held the door open for me did I realize that he was me.

How do you mean? asked Lena. We had reached the end of the gravel path, and were standing in front of a big, ocher cube that was adjoining the Grecian portico. In a funny voice she read the sign on the wall that enclosed the building, a Swedish word that after some puzzling we concluded must mean Resurrection Chapel. Next to the chapel was a long low building that housed washrooms and had various other metal doors. Do you suppose the dead are laid out here? asked Lena, laying her palm on one of the doors. Do you think someone's lying there, waiting to be resurrected? Her expression was one of mock horror. Where shall we go? I asked. I don't care, she said. But I don't want to turn back. We chose a direction at random and strolled slowly on through the rows of graves.

What did you mean, that you were him? Lena asked me again. Hard to explain, I said. As soon as I clapped eyes on the young man I knew that he and I were one and the same. Because you'd worked there as a night porter before? Not just that, I said. It was like looking into a mirror. Amazingly, he seemed to have no sense of the resemblance, of the identity. He gave me a perfectly ordinary greeting, and walked ahead of me to the reception desk, handed me my key, and said good night.

It took me a long time to get to sleep that night. I kept thinking of the night porter, and how he was now the one walking round the unlit spaces, and it felt to me as though I was there with him, and I had the mixture of fear and excitement I had then, when I was doing my rounds. My predecessor had been an old man, who explained and demonstrated everything to me in the course of two or three nights. The main hotel entrance had to be locked at midnight, and then there were the security rounds, doors to lock and lights to turn off. While doing that I also had to do a few further chores, all in all not more than a couple of hours. I swept the yard, sorted the empty bottles in the restaurant, admitted the odd returning guest. At two or three in the morning, I would help myself to something from the kitchen fridges. After that I could have lain down on a little put-me-up bed behind the reception desk, but I never slept; instead, I read or gambled away my wages on the slot machine beside the entrance. Sometimes I even aimlessly wandered around, took in my surroundings, a place of strangeness in the middle of the familiar village. It was a place of travelers

who met like the members of a secret sect, unnoticed by
the villagers. Shortly after four, the driver who supplied
the local kiosks with newspapers and magazines would
rap on the door. I let him in and got each of us a coffee
from the machine. The driver was a nice man who'd had
a difficult life that he would tell me about in his soft voice
night after night. Soon after he left, the day porter would
turn up. I was still living at home, and would breakfast
with my parents, for whom the day was just beginning,
even as mine was coming to an end. Usually I would just
sleep till noon or so. I can well remember my curious
afternoons when I felt simultaneously very tired and
strangely alert, that sense of having fallen out of time,
and following my own irregular rhythm.

I had meant to go back early the next morning, but
by the time I was out of bed, I had to hurry so as not
to miss breakfast. There was a young woman sitting at
the reception desk now, and for a moment I wondered
if I had just imagined my nocturnal encounter with my
other self, or maybe dreamed it.

My book was selling well, and I toured around a lot, giving readings and being interviewed. I even had some foreign deals, and corresponded with translators and publishers abroad, and got invited to literary festivals in other countries. I was awarded a scholarship, by my standards a vast sum that would permit me to live frugally for over a year. But no amount of success could blind me to the fact that I had no idea what to write next. I kept embarking on new projects, only to abandon them after a couple of dozen pages in boredom and irritation. It wasn't just that I had no ideas, my language was stale, maybe because writing wasn't a necessity for me, just an obligation. There were times I didn't write a word for weeks, killing time reading or vaguely researching some project I ended up ditching anyway. I was still living in the apartment I had shared with my girlfriend. Everything reminded me of her, and happy as I was about my literary success, I suffered just as much from the loss of my girlfriend.

My encounter that night wouldn't leave me. One time, I even called the hotel and asked after the night porter, but my description of him was so sketchy, and my purported reasons for making the inquiry so threadbare, that the woman on the phone got suspicious, and asked me what was my name again, and then stopped talking altogether. I started writing about my doppelgänger; as with my first book it wasn't so much the attempt to write a literary text, as a desire to fathom what had happened. This time, though, I wasn't successful, the story was too eccentric and peculiar for me to be able to grasp it.

I thought a lot about my girlfriend, read the letters we had exchanged, looked at the photos of the holidays we'd taken together. We'd had hardly any money, but still we'd got around a lot, went hitchhiking and on walking holidays, slept in youth hostels or tents. She was an actress, and often had weeks off between engagements. We were happy together, even if I might wonder what she saw in me, and what I did to deserve her. We were together for three years; even so, she remained in many respects an enigma to me.

I'm an actor too, said Lena. I know, I said. How do you know? she asked. What makes you claim you know everything about me? Have you been snooping? No, I said, I wouldn't call it that. I have no idea why I'm even listening to this, she said. Maybe because you're curious? Lena shook her head a little, as though surprised at herself. I hate it when someone pursues me. But I don't think that's what you're doing. This isn't about me, is it?

We had got to the end of the cemetery and had left it behind us and carried on, first through a part of town with modest wooden houses, then another section with blocks of flats. Between the blocks were densely planted trees. In some places, the granite poked through the earth, as though to shrug off the thin layer of civilization. It wasn't four o'clock yet, but it was already starting to get dark.

Shall we stop for coffee? suggested Lena. I was happy to do that, and after a bit, we found a bakery with a few plastic chairs and tables. We got cups of watery coffee at the counter and sat down in the big plate-glass window that was blinded by steam and still had Christmas decorations stuck to it, a Santa Claus sitting on a sleigh drawn by reindeer, laden with parcels. For the first time, Lena seemed properly aware of me. She looked directly at me, smiled, and said, Crazy story. It's a long way from over, I said, and carried on.

My book had been out for almost a year when a professor at my old university invited me to take part in a seminar on contemporary Swiss literature. He asked me to read aloud to his class, and to tell them about my writing. I was glad of the distraction and spent far too much time over the little talk I meant to give.

It was a rainy day in late March, the seminar met in the late afternoon. The college premises were little changed since my own time there, students still sat around cross-legged on the cold stone floors in the hallways, and the bulletin boards were full of posters announcing various courses and lecture topics and student politics, only the coffee seemed to have gotten better. I thought about the boredom during the lectures, and the dozy hours spent in the library. I had spent weeks writing up various papers, in the knowledge that no more than two or three people would ever read them, a thought that was both comforting and discouraging. I could no longer imagine what it was that had driven me in those days. I hadn't been idle, but in my memory those years were characterized by a profound indecisiveness. I'd been trapped inside that warren of university buildings as in a labyrinth, with the difference that it held no terrors for me, but rather gave me a sense of security. All the images I retained in my mind from that time were dim, as though lit by low-watt lightbulbs.

The professor's seminar seemed to enjoy considerable popularity. It was held in a large lecture hall. When I stepped in, there were already at least forty students sitting on the benches; just like in my day, more women than men. While the professor gave a brief introduction, I looked around and suddenly saw him, the night porter, the younger version of myself. He was sitting by the aisle most of the way back and was holding a plastic cup that he sipped out of from time to time. The sight of him so utterly disoriented me that I no longer heard what the professor was saying. Only when there was an expectant silence did I realize he must have finished and given me the floor. I got a grip on myself and started on my talk, in which I compared writing to the search for a path in an unfamiliar landscape, and posited the difference between the private and the autobiographical. There were questions afterwards. The young man from my village seemed to have been paying close attention, each time I looked up at him our eyes would meet, and I quickly looked away, as though he might otherwise recognize me and give me away. He didn't ask a question, just made occasional notes in a small notebook that he tucked away in his pocket each time. After the bell rang, the professor said a few words by way of conclusion and reminded those present of the author who was due the following week. I wasn't surprised that my double was one of the first to leave the lecture theater, with hurried steps, as though he had another class to go to. I had half a mind to follow him, but a few students ringed me with books to sign, one young woman asked me for a piece for the student magazine, and another wanted advice in finding a publisher. By the time everyone went away satisfied, the young man was long gone. I asked the professor if he knew him. Brown hair like mine, a plastic coffee cup in his hand, sixth or seventh row, far left. He couldn't place him. Probably a freshman, he said, they come and go, I can't possibly know them all.

The following week, I visited the German department again, waiting in the hallway for the seminar to finish. No sooner had the bell gone this time than there was my double running down the steps. I followed him out of the building and along the street. He only had a sweater on, even though it was cool and rainy. He headed in the direction of the lake, turned off at the theater, and zigzagged through the lanes of the old town to an old-fashioned café I had often patronized myself in my time as a student.

The place was almost empty. I sat down at a table behind him. The waitress took his order, a toasted sandwich and a small beer. I'll have the same, I said, when she approached. She looked at me in bewilderment, and I repeated his order. He didn't seem to hear, because he had taken down a newspaper from a rack by the door and was leafing through it. I went and helped myself to one as well, but I couldn't concentrate on any of the articles because I kept squinnying across to him.

It was as though a playmate had copied my every word when I was a child, copied every movement, which used to put me into a seething rage. Now too I had the feeling that the other party was copying me, my way of crossing my legs, of folding the newspaper, of adjusting the silverware on the table. He used my words to thank the waitress, ate his toasted sandwich as slowly and carefully as I did. When he was finished, he pushed his plate back, took a big notebook out of his rucksack, and started to read in it. Sometimes he would cross things out, or write something in with a fine push pencil of the kind I had once favored myself. I made a few notes too, but when I read them back to myself later, it was just confused stuff.

At the end of an hour or so, the student paid and left. For a brief moment I thought of speaking to him, but I found a strange reluctance, even timidity. I paid in turn and trailed him through deserted streets and lanes. I knew this quarter very well and wasn't at all surprised to see him walk into the building I had once had an attic room in as a student. On the top bell was my name in a script that was the spit of mine.

Three young women had come in and sat down at the next table, each of them with a baby monitor. Look at that, said Lena, pointing to the three baby carriages parked outside in the cold, they're getting their kids used to the fact that life is no bundle of laughs. I don't think it's possible to get used to cold, I said.

Lena stood up and took our empty cups back to the counter. On her return, she stopped and looked at me briefly. There are simple explanations for everything, she said in a cheery voice. What's that then? I asked. You're mad, and this is all a product of your imagination. In that case you'd better go back to your hotel, I said. I'm not scared of you, she said. I want to hear how the story ends first. I can't tell you the end of the story, I said, the only stories that have endings are the ones in books. But I can tell you what happened next.

Neither of us knew where we were, so we just decided to go on in the same direction, wherever that led us.

This second encounter with my doppelgänger threw me for a loop, I said. Once again, I tried to make a story out of what had happened, but whatever I tried or wrote, I had the feeling someone was standing behind me, making fun of me. My whole life seemed ridiculous and false. When I thought about telling my girlfriend I loved her, I seemed to hear the other fellow saying the same thing to his girlfriend like an echo from the future. His words sounded as though they'd been taken from a cheap romance. When I remembered how we used to kiss, I saw him and her kissing. I was jealous of him, it was as though he was stealing my memories by reliving them. At the same time, I could feel, years before he first met my girlfriend, how he would lose her again. But the worst thing was that I started to question my love and hers, and everything that had happened between us. Our whole history felt like a failed rehearsal for a theatrical flop.

EIGHT

EIGHT

In the meantime, it had gotten completely dark. We had negotiated a rather disagreeable neighborhood crisscrossed by wide highways, had crossed a high bridge, and at last entered a long shopping street. The buildings on either side were identical, most of the businesses were international chains, we could have been anywhere. As we walked slowly on, people passed us and we passed others who were probably coming off work and were on their way home. Lena linked arms with me, as though afraid of getting lost in the crowd.

I know the feeling, she said. Sometimes, when I can't find my way into a part, I can watch myself act, and then it feels like I'm not playing the part, the part is playing me, as though the character were aping me, and poking fun at me. I don't think the audience notices anything, but I can feel all the strength draining out of me, as if I was just an empty shell at the end of the performance, a costume that needs to be hung up till the next time.

But I missed my girlfriend so badly, I said, I sometimes had the feeling I was half a person, as though I couldn't exist without her. Did you say that to her? Lena asked me with an urgency that surprised me. Did you try to win her back? I didn't reply. Lena let go of my arm and stopped. When I turned towards her she looked at me sharply and said, I don't think he's anything like you. No, he really isn't. And it's not such an unusual name as all that either. Anyway, everyone calls my boyfriend Chris. No one ever called me that, I said. And he doesn't have writer's block either, said Lena, walking on, he's working and he's doing well. What's he writing about then? I asked, though I already knew the answer. He doesn't like to talk about things he's working on currently, she said. Then how do you know he's actually writing anything? He's almost at the end, she said, it's a very special project. He's writing about you, isn't he, I said. What if he is? said Lena.

NINE

NINE

Back then, it had been Magdalena's idea. I had just dropped one of my more ambitious projects and was this close to quitting writing altogether. I complained to her how everything I wrote seemed artificial and constructed, any story I think up has been told hundreds of times, and better than I could ever do it, too. Write about something that's near to you, she said. Write from your feelings, not your head. Tell your own story. I don't have a story, I said, my childhood was as unique as every other childhood, my youth was no more traumatic than anyone else's. And my life now? Do you want me to write a book about a guy who can't get it together to write a book? Write a book about you and me, about our life, our love. Your ideas are a bit simplistic, I said, a literary text needs form and consequence, and our life doesn't, you don't get good stories made out of happiness.

But the next time Magdalena went away for a week to rehearse, I did indeed start writing about her, little scenes from our life together, more images than· stories. How we tested out beds in a furniture store, and the sales assistant looked at her as though he wouldn't mind trying it on with her, how we painted the kitchen, and we got drunk on the paint fumes, how one rainy day we didn't manage to get out of bed, and then we did, and I found myself running to the bakery, with drizzle in my face, and I suddenly thought about running off somewhere, even though I was happier than I had ever been in my life. How we went walking in the mountains and were caught up in a storm, and I suddenly understood we could die, in fact that one day we would die.

On the weekend Magdalena came home and asked what I'd done while she'd been away. Oh, this and that, I said. I didn't tell her anything about what I'd written about her. It felt as though I'd betrayed her with my image of her, as though the written Magdalena was more important to me than the living woman. I looked at her, and no longer knew her, and yet I had the feeling I could see her with more realism than ever, a wholly alien woman. What's the matter? she asked, looking worried. I shook my head and embraced her, as though I could get closer to her that way.

———————

So she's got the same name as me? put in Lena. Yes, I said crustily, her name's Magdalena, like yours. Tell me about her. What's there to tell? I loved her. How did you meet her? asked Lena. In the mountains, I said, glancing at her, but she looked expressionlessly at me, and said, go on.

We were staying in the same hotel, a little pension in the Engadin. Magdalena was with a group of people who went hiking in the daytime, and every evening kept the guests amused with stories and comic turns. I noticed her because she was quieter than the others, but she still seemed to be the focus of things. She was by some way the youngest of the group, and all three of the men were after her, but in such an eccentric way that the other women didn't seem to mind.

I had gone up into the mountains to write my novel. At that time, I still had the notion that you could work better in a quieter setting. I spent most of the time sitting at a little granite table in the shady garden of the hotel, writing or reading, just the way you'd expect of a writer. When I came down to breakfast one morning, the group was just about to set out. They discussed the plan for the day noisily, but this time their cheeriness sounded forced, and when they finally left the dining room, Magdalena was left behind on her own.

Later, I went into the hotel garden to work, and I found her sitting at my table, with a handful of papers. I just managed to glance at them, and guessed it was a theater script. She must have sensed my hesitation. Is this your place? she asked. Stay where you are, I said, I'll find another table. She pointed to the chair opposite and said, You're welcome to sit by me.

I tried to work, but it was more than I could do, I kept glancing across to her. Then she looked up from her papers, as though sensing my regard, and smiled at me. Are you keeping a diary? she asked finally. At that time I felt a little ashamed of my scribbling; much as I'd have liked to be a successful author, I felt at least as much ashamed of being a failure. Oh, just notes, I said. I keep a diary, she said, I write in it almost every day. Have done since I was eleven. What do you write? I asked. All kinds of things. What I'm doing, people I meet, things that are preoccupying me. Do you think I've got a chance of appearing in your diary, then? I asked. Only if you have a coffee with me, she said, and held out her hand. Magdalena. The whole scene had a touch of formality about it, which she seemed to enjoy. I went inside to place the order.

Now you're going to have to say or do something extraordinary, said Magdalena with a smile, once I was back, so that you'll cut a good figure in my diary. She laid the script face down on the table so that I couldn't see the title, and looked at me expectantly. Why didn't you go off with the others? I asked. She paused, as though wondering if it was worth telling me the reason. That's another story, she finally said. It's not interesting. We're actors. Next week we're going to start rehearsing a play. Before that we wanted to spend a few days in the mountains to get to know each other a bit. The director said he thought it would help us to bond. Probably didn't work. She shrugged. And now I'm sitting here, bored. Would you like to go walking with me?

We finished our coffee and arranged to meet outside the hotel in fifteen minutes. When Magdalena showed up half an hour later, I was just studying the signpost, which had arrows pointing every which way. But it turned out she already knew which way she wanted to go, and pointed up the slope behind us, and said it was too steep for the others.

The path led straight up through a larch wood. We walked silently in Indian file, only speaking the few times we stopped to catch our breath. At the end of an hour or so, we reached the timberline. The path led up to a scree that formed a great hollow. By now we had been walking for over two hours, and we sat down on a rock to rest. All I had with me was a bottle of water, I had had no idea that what Magdalena had in mind was a proper mountain hike. It was a hot summer's day, and I was bathed in sweat. Magdalena was delicate and slightly built, but she seemed to be less exhausted than me, and before long she was pressing to carry on.

Fully three hours after setting off, we reached a tiny lake in a dip in the rocks. Magdalena was intent on reaching a nearby summit whose name she liked. And half an hour later, we duly got there, and the landscape opened out below us, the valley and the lakes down in the depths, and across from us a chain of snow-covered peaks.

ELEVEN

ELEVEN

Then on the way back we bathed in the lake, said Lena. I was surprised by Chris's pallor, and he was amazed at my lack of inhibition. The water was ice cold, we just dipped into it, then lay down naked on some rocks to get dry.

She stopped and looked me in the eye. A young man who had been hard on her heels almost walked into her and said something unfriendly-sounding in Swedish. It's all in his book, she said. I don't know how you got to see the text, but the fact that you know it proves nothing. I didn't read it, I said, I wrote it. Almost twenty years ago. In that case, you can tell me how the story continues, she said. I could at that, the question is whether you'd want to hear it. Without another word, she walked off down the street. When I had caught up to her, she said triumphantly, Anyway, I never bathed in the lake. It was his idea, but I never dreamed of undressing in front of him.

He said he just wanted to cool off quickly. I went on. He thought he would catch me up, but he was mistaken about that.

It was our first trial of strength, and Magdalena won it, the way she won almost all our battles later on as well. When I walked into the restaurant that evening, she was sitting around a table with her theater friends. I nodded to her, but she just gave me a mocking smile. Later, I ran into one of the men smoking in the hotel garden. It turned out he was the author of the play they were going to produce. I asked him when and where they were having the premiere, but he didn't seem to want to talk to me. When I went back inside, I ran into Magdalena. She greeted me like a perfect stranger.

I left the light off in my room and went up to the window. Out in the garden I could see the outlines of two people standing close together, and I was almost certain it was Magdalena and the playwright. They seemed to be talking, then they embraced and started kissing. I felt violently jealous, not just of their love, but of their life and the world they moved in and seemed to belong in.

That night I couldn't sleep for a long time. When I went downstairs just before ten o'clock the next morning, the theater group were just carrying down their luggage and stowing it in a taxi.

You can ask me anything you like, I said. Not just what's in the book, but also what actually happened. Why should I? asked Lena. You've got your life, and I've got mine. And I've no intention of letting you tell me mine.

We were walking on, now in the old town, whose crowded streets made it difficult to talk. Lena looked at the window displays and saw a plain blue dress she liked and was desperate to try on. I went into the shop with her and told her how lovely she looked, as though she wouldn't have been lovely to me in any other dress. I offered to buy it for her, but she insisted on paying for it herself. For the first time she seemed seriously annoyed. Just because I'm listening to you doesn't mean you can take liberties with me. I'm not your Magdalena and don't intend to become it either. I apologized and said I hadn't meant any harm. She walked out of the shop and briefly stopped. I was already half-afraid she wanted to run off and had no idea what I could do to stop her. Finally, she walked on, and I followed her in silence, so as not to make her angry a second time.

Only when we had left the city center did we start talking again. We were walking through a section of characterless gray tenements. There were lights on in many of the windows, and in some of the lower stories you could see people going about their domestic tasks. One man who was standing on a balcony smoking gave us a wave and called out something I couldn't understand.

Whenever I look into an apartment, I imagine what it would be like to live in it, said Lena. She was back to sounding like before. A new life in a new city. I would have a different job, maybe a husband and children, a dog, I'd play tennis, or take courses at a local technical college. Don't you always slip into the skin of your characters when you play a part? I asked. I don't mean it in that way, said Lena, I mean a completely different life, a different history. Tell me about being in love, said Lena, how did you fall in love with her? Love isn't really the word, I said. I liked Magdalena, she fascinated me and challenged me, but it took me some time to fall in love with her. You see, said Lena, Chris fell in love with me right away. It really was love at first sight.

Maybe I believed that to begin with, but after everything that happened later, I had a different sense of the story. In writing, I was cautious with big words and sentiments, questioning them not only in others, but also in myself. I had liked Magdalena from the first, but that was hardly surprising, she was young and beautiful, and she had a lightness that straightaway charmed everyone and won them over. On our walk, it was usually her going on ahead, and I had plenty of opportunities to watch her. Her movements were swift, as though she was in a lighter atmosphere or somewhere almost without gravity. She was wearing climbing boots, but her footfall was light, almost skipping. She kept turning around to face me and smiling and calling out words of encouragement, but when she felt my eyes weren't on her, her expression was serious, almost dismissive. Sometimes it felt like seeing the face of the old woman she would one day become.

Love at first sight, I said. Looking back, you believe that kind of thing, when you find your narrative, settle on a version, a creation myth for your relationship. Because that's always the easiest thing to believe, and the pleasantest. That you were destined for each other, that there was no other possibility. But if I hadn't happened to see a poster for the play two months later, in all probability I'd have forgotten the whole thing, just like I've forgotten lots of other beginnings.

When I saw Magdalena again, this time on the stage, first I didn't recognize her. She was playing a rather foolish young woman who senses that her boyfriend is still in love with his ex, and who is then seduced by the ex's husband. I couldn't really remember the play, all I knew for sure was that there was a fish on the poster.

That figures into the play as well, said Lena, it's a carp that slowly asphyxiates. It's night. The middle of a lake. I am floating on the water. It's snowing, and the snowflakes fall into the water and dissolve. I have to be naked, but I don't feel cold. There is no greater feeling of abandon. Then suddenly I see that underneath me, facing me like a shadow, is a gigantic fish in the water. Is that in the play? I asked, I can't remember.

He paid me, said Lena. In the play, I mean. The man didn't seduce me, he offered me money to sleep with him. Not like a prostitute, though. He said that was the purest form of love, when you own someone. Because that way love isn't based on reciprocity, loving someone just to be loved in return. Do you think that's right? I asked. Nonsense, she said. I don't want to possess anyone or be possessed by them. What about being obsessed by them, then? It's more like having someone obsessed with me, said Lena. That's what I said to Chris right off the bat, when he was waiting for me at the stage door. I don't like that. But you stayed and had a glass of wine with him anyway? Why shouldn't I? said Lena.

THIRTEEN

We had gone to an expensive bar, not far from the theater. I couldn't think of a more suitable place, and Magdalena seemed happy to be taken to somewhere ritzy like
that. Even the barman seemed to sense it was a special
moment for us. There were lots of people in the bar, but
he still seemed to treat us as though we were the stars
of the evening. The bill for two drinks was ridiculous,
but spending so much money gave the moment a significance that put me into an almost solemn mood.

I made a couple of remarks about the play and the
production. Magdalena already seemed to be slightly fed
up with her part, and she didn't feel like hashing out the
production with me either. I asked her about the playwright, tried to sense how she stood with him, if she was
still in touch with him, but she didn't react to that either,
and her answers were monosyllabic. She was altogether
rather quiet, and I too was quieter and quieter, perhaps

that's why I soon had a sense of intimacy. Eventually, Magdalena pressed against the bar with both hands, leaned back on her stool, and asked if I'd walk her home.

She lived on the outskirts of the city, we could have taken a streetcar, but she insisted on walking. As we wandered through the empty streets, we started to talk. We talked about the city and its inhabitants, about our lives and our backgrounds, we got to talking about her part, and about love and possession. The play threw up more questions than answers, and we talked about whether it was wrong to love someone for their looks. What happens when I lose my looks, then? asked Magdalena. By some accident or illness or just over the course of time. Will you still love me then? That would be true love, I said, that isn't determined by external factors. I'm not sure. But the way I look is an aspect of me, said Magdalena. And if my looks change, then part of me changes too. Why shouldn't that affect your love? Suddenly she laughed. That's my favorite part of the play. The bit where I tell my boyfriend that the other man paid me to have sex with him, and he asks, How much? He just wants to know how much I'm worth to the other man. You have to be Swiss to ask a question like that.

At the end of almost two hours, Magdalena finally stopped in front of a gray Fifties tenement, thanked me for my company, gave me a peck on the cheek, and said if I liked, I could walk her home another time.

FOURTEEN

I never asked him if he would still love me when I lost my looks, said Lena, I put the question in a general way. But that was how he took it, I said. And when we said goodbye, he tried to kiss me on the lips, but I turned my head away. A bit late, I said. So what happens when I lose my looks? asked Lena. Does he still love me? You're just as beautiful as you were then, I said. I'm not talking about you, I'm asking about Chris and me, said Lena.

For some time now, we'd been walking along a road with heavy traffic, lined with industrial premises, warehouses and workshops, and in one place an auto repair shop with a closed gas station. Next to it was a big yard full of used cars. I need to pee, said Lena. There's a light up ahead, I said, and sure enough after a couple of hundred yards, we got to a brightly lit furniture megastore that was still open. We seemed to be the only customers. When a solitary sales assistant asked me what we were looking for, I claimed to be interested in a reading chair, while Lena vanished in search of the ladies' room. The assistant showed me various designs and explained their qualities in uncertain English. After a few minutes Lena came back, linked arms with me, and said, Have you forgotten, darling, we wanted to buy a bed. And to the sales assistant she said, You must know, we're newly married and we need a solidly built bed, but my husband's too inhibited to ask. The sales assistant shook his head in puzzlement and said, Beds are on the third floor. But remember, we close in twenty minutes, he said, pointing us the way to the elevators, and we thanked him.

The bed department had little bays with suggested arrangements on display, simulated bedrooms with beds and cabinets and wall cupboards. Lena stopped in front of a four-poster in the colonial style, with white tulle curtains. On either side were suitable stands and huge wrought-iron candelabra with golden candles. On the thin partition that separated this room from its neighbor hung a painting of a fairy-tale forest, with a great stag peacefully grazing in it. Sweet dreams, said Lena, laughing. If I were a little deerling, I'd walk into the forest clearing . . . Can you imagine the kind of people who'd buy a bedroom like that? With a few words, gestures, and facial expressions, she played the woman begging her husband for such a suite. Oh, darling, she said, can't we, please! I always wanted a four-poster.

There was no sales staff to be seen anywhere, and it felt eerie to be walking through this sequence of unlived-in projections of possible lives that all looked alike in their sterility. In the next bay were rustic pine items, and Lena turned into a gifted mother and housewife, explaining to me in fantasy Swedish how easy it all was to assemble and keep clean, and how we could turn the bunk bed into two singles once our children were old enough, and each wanted a room of their own. How many kids have we got again? I asked. Two, of course, she said, a boy and a girl, as is only right and proper. The next bay saw her as a businesswoman, praising the cool design of the tubular steel furniture, and testing all the drawers for ease of use and fit. Then last of all she was the beguiling seductress, settling herself on the red velvet coverlet of a bedroom that was all black lacquer and mirrors, beckoning to me with one finger. I sat down next to her and asked which of these women she most resembled. Which one would you like? she asked. Before I could answer, she said, But they're all clichés, just like the respective bedrooms. If there was a bra lying on the floor and a cat on the bed and a book of crossword puzzles on the bedside table and a packet of sleeping tablets, that would make a story. You could hear the water rushing in the shower, I said, and through the open window, the sounds of the city beyond. It would have to be a different city, said Lena, it had better be America. The curtains would billow in the wind. And when did we kiss for the first time? she asked. That wasn't till months later, I said.

FIFTEEN

FIFTEEN

Now I was collecting Magdalena after the show as often as I could. Each time she chose a different route, and it wasn't unusual for us to lose our way in quiet residential districts, going on long detours, and taking an hour longer than the night before. But since at that time I was working as a freelance copywriter for an advertising agency and didn't have to get up early, I didn't care how late it got. If we happened to pass a bar on the way that was still open, we would have a beer or a glass of wine, and sometimes fell into conversation with some night birds, loners, or drunks who would tell us their stories. Once, we even blundered into a wedding party, and a couple of drunken guests who had stepped out to smoke took us back inside with them, introduced us to the bride and groom, and didn't let up till we had eaten a piece of wedding cake. When we finally left, one of the guests made a present to Magdalena of the bride's bouquet, but she gave it back, saying she didn't feel like getting married, and they should find another victim.

Magdalena didn't let me into her apartment until one time in spring, when she was sick. She had just started rehearsing a new play when she called me one morning and said she had a cold, and did I feel like visiting her.

She opened the door in her nightie, and asked me in. Her cheeks had this hectic red, as though she'd put on too much rouge, otherwise she looked perfectly normal. Will you make me a cup of tea? she asked, and led me down a dark corridor to the kitchen. You will find everything by yourself, won't you? Just look around, she said. I'm going back to bed. When I started opening the cupboards, I had the sense I was doing something unlawful. I found what I needed, put water on to boil, and went into the living room. Her furniture looked like it had come out of charity shops, but it was well chosen and well matched. It was all in the style of the Fifties and Sixties, only her big bookcase was a cheap standard product, the kind of thing you see everywhere. I was amazed how many books Magdalena seemed to have. They were arranged alphabetically by author, most of them hardback, and presumably, again, secondhand. There were a lot of classics, entire editions of Goethe and Gottfried Keller and others, but some more recent stuff too, tattered paperback copies of Celan and Bachmann, Hemingway and Kafka.

I could hear the kettle whistling in the kitchen, and I went back and made the tea. I went into the bedroom

with two steaming mugs, and there was Magdalena
sitting bolt upright in bed, looking expectantly at me.
Once again, I was struck by her red cheeks and her voice,
which sounded breathy and a little lower than usual. I
don't know why, but I had the sense she was just pretend-
ing to be ill. The whole setup seemed to me to be a sort
of game I didn't understand the purpose of. At the same
time, I couldn't shake the feeling that Magdalena was
testing me. She watched my every move, occasionally
correcting me or adjusting something, as though there
was only one way of moving the books on the bedside
table or drawing the curtains; as though the mugs had to
be on one particular spot, and in a certain fixed relation
to one another. At last she let herself fall back into the
pillows with a satisfied expression. Is everything the way
you like it now? I asked.

She said she had her new part to learn, but she had
a headache, and her concentration was poor, and could I
perhaps help her? She reached under the bed and pulled
up a sheaf of paper and passed it to me. There, you read
the man. Only the parts where he's talking with Julie.
We don't need the rest. What about stage directions? She
shook her head. Okay, begin.

Miss Julie's gone mad again tonight, completely mad!
I read. No, not that, said Magdalena, he says that to
Christine. She took the script out of my hand, turned a
couple of pages ahead, and pointed to a place. Here.

Have you ladies secrets to discuss? I read. Magdalena took a paper handkerchief out of the packet next to her on the bed and swished it around in front of me. Don't be inquisitive! Ah! Charming, that smell of violets, I read. Impertinent! said Magdalena flirtatiously, So you know about perfumes, too? You certainly know how to dance...She got up, walked around to the back of my chair, and laid her hands on my shoulders. Come now, and dance a schottische with me, Jean. I don't wish to seem disrespectful..., I read. I am the lady of the house, said Magdalena, and when I take the floor I want to dance with someone who knows how to lead. That's not what it says here, I said, looking up at her. She looked as though she was utterly furious with me, and she was gripping my shoulders so hard it hurt.

SIXTEEN

SIXTEEN

Lena had lain down on the bed and shut her eyes, and she looked like a little girl daydreaming. I grazed her shoulder, and she sat up and asked me what I was thinking. About Magdalena, I said. What about you?

A man in a blue uniform walked down the passageway. He seemed astonished to see us, said something in Swedish, and when we looked at him uncomprehendingly, in English. The store was about to close, hadn't we heard the announcements? He escorted us to the elevators and stood there till we had got into one. Too bad, said Lena, as we descended. It really was cozy up there. Have you ever written for the theater? Television, I said. Lena led the way to the exit, where the sales assistant stood whom we'd seen before. As he unlocked the door for us, he wished us a pleasant evening and all the luck. Perhaps he had really believed Lena when she said we were newlyweds.

The first time we kissed was back at her house, I said, once we were standing outside the store. She was unwell. I helped her learn a part, Miss Julie, by August Strindberg. Lena said nothing.

We walked on down the street, more slowly now than before, it felt as though we were in a dream world in which all things were possible, but nothing mattered. I still love you, I finally said, quietly. First I thought Lena hadn't heard me, but after a while she said: You love your Magdalena, not me. We don't even know each other. I said, the Magdalena I was in love with was like you, young and beautiful and carefree. If a man finds me young and beautiful and carefree and nothing else, then I'd better start running, said Lena. I don't know what she's like today, I said, what she looks like. Perhaps she's long since forgotten me. Nonsense, said Lena, she won't have forgotten you, whatever transpired between the two of you. I wanted to talk to you yesterday, I said. I stood outside your hotel, but when I saw you, I felt so overcome that I couldn't do it. It was even more of a shock than when I first saw my doppelgänger. I followed you all afternoon, for at least a couple of hours I wanted to live in the illusion that I was young again and could give my life a different turn.

SEVENTEEN

SEVENTEEN

Even when I saw Lena onstage, I was shocked by her resemblance to Magdalena. But when she walked out of the hotel and stopped a few feet away from me, it took my breath away, and I felt paralyzed. She hesitated briefly, looked up and down the street, then, seemingly at random but nonetheless purposefully, she struck out for the center. She was walking fast and, barely stopping to think, I set off after her. She looked just like my Magdalena when she accompanied me to Stockholm sixteen years ago now, with a swaying, almost skipping walk, and the same facial expression, a mixture of astonishment and amusement. Sometimes she would suddenly crane her neck and look up, as though she had heard something or was looking for something, then her expression became serious, and for a moment it was as though she was listening out for something only she could hear.

We had been together for three years, sometime I had left my old apartment and moved in with her. By now she wasn't attached to a particular theater anymore, and I was only rarely turning out copy for the ad agency and was starting to write for newspapers and magazines instead. I had never quite given up the desire to write seriously, though I didn't do much to realize it either. The text about Magdalena and my life hadn't seemed to lead anywhere. Eventually I told her about it, claiming our life was too uneventful for it to be made into literature. Why write it all down? I asked, after all, we're living it. In reality I was afraid of Magdalena becoming a stranger to me again, and that the fictive Magdalena could supplant the real one. Magdalena seemed to be happy that I'd given up the idea. She encouraged me instead to write dramatic texts, with parts in them that she could play. But I didn't seem to be able to manage that either. I like you best when you're not playing a part, I said. It was true, I didn't enjoy seeing her onstage, because I didn't want to have to see that she was capable of being a completely different person, that our love was not the only possibility in her.

Even when we were alone together, I sometimes had the sense that she was playing a part, maybe not deliberately, but because she couldn't help it. Perhaps it was that that wouldn't let me go, the feeling I could never get really close to her, never see through her, never possess her. I puzzled over what I might be to her. The only certain proof of her love was that she stayed with me. When we went to parties or premieres together, she was swarmed by men who were better-looking than me, who were cleverer and funnier and above all more successful and had more to offer her than I did. She would flirt a little with one or other of them, but sooner or later she would always come to me and say she had had enough, and could we go home now. There was something painful and consuming about my love for her. Even when we were living together, I sometimes had palpitations when she came home later than she'd said, and suddenly stood there in the apartment, as though setting foot there for the first time.

One day Magdalena showed me an advertisement in the paper. They were looking for television writers for a new series. That would be something for us, don't you think? You write the scripts, and I'll play the leads. We'll be rich and famous, like Marilyn Monroe and Arthur Miller. Well, you know what happened to them, I said, but nevertheless I applied. I devised a couple of plots, wrote some trial scenes and sent them to the producer. I was invited to meet them, and was told my ideas were not filmable, but they saw some potential in my writing anyway. I got to work again, and proposed a series set in a meteorological research station in the Alps. For a few months, I was in regular back-and-forth with the TV people. They kept pressing me to more commercial subjects, sent me examples of screenplays they liked, and gradually cut everything from my scenes that I thought was original or clever. At least I wasn't badly paid for the work, and eventually, along with a director and an editor, I got an invitation to participate in a master class in Stockholm, to be led by an American TV writer.

I had hoped to maybe see a bit of the city, instead I spent whole days with writers from half of Europe cooped up in the conference room of an anonymous hotel, listening to the American hold forth about story lines and plot points, and trying to get us going with his phony enthusiasm. No one can stop you now except you yourselves, he said, and passed around memos of tips and tricks and claimed that if you only followed his advice you would become a celebrated TV writer. I asked myself what such a man was doing leading workshops in so-so hotels in Sweden if he was that clued into the secrets of successful scripts. Everything was getting me down, the yammering American, the participants who eagerly took down his every word, the two TV people there with me who treated me as the tyro I suppose I was. Magdalena spent her days in the city and when we met up at the end of the afternoon, told me what she had been up to. In the evening all the workshop participants, plus leader, ate dinner together. The first evening Magdalena joined us, but she seemed to be even more bored than me, and when we got up to our room at midnight, told me one author was plenty for her, she would eat dinner alone tomorrow, and maybe take herself to the theater or the cinema.

While I was trailing Lena, I had asked myself whether someone might have followed my Magdalena sixteen years ago; if not only did I have a doppelgänger, but I might be someone else's, links in an endless chain of identical lives running through time. I tried to remember what Magdalena had told me about how she spent her days, whether she had visited the forest cemetery with a man who had told her some crazy story. But would she even have told me? Would she have believed him? Did Lena believe me?

She went into a few stores, looked at dresses, shoes, furnishings. She bought a red rocking horse, a couple of glass candleholders, and a T-shirt bearing the legend I ♥ SWEDISH GIRLS. She ate her lunch at a small café. Afraid to lose her from sight, I waited outside and watched through the window as she conducted a laughing conversation with the waitress, who then gestured, as though to point her the way. After lunch, Lena chose her direction with even greater purpose, and led me to the Nationalmuseum, a classical building facing the water.

There were very few visitors, and I followed her through the quiet rooms. The pictures were hung densely, often one over the other, and some of the rooms contained sculptures and partition walls with even more paintings hung on them. Lena didn't seem to be that interested in art. She crossed the rooms without stopping, as though absolving a show-jumping course, or on the lookout for something or someone. The only time she stopped was in front of a few still lifes. After she had moved on, I stopped to look at the pictures, which were by a Dutch seventeenth-century master, and depicted the cannily arranged booty of successful hunting expeditions, dead foxes, game birds, and hares. One picture showed a couple of hounds, and another a cat stretching out her claws in the direction of the dead birds.

Lena had gone on, but I caught up to her quickly enough. She had sat down on a bench a couple of rooms farther on, looking abstractedly in front of her. She seemed not to have noticed that anyone else was in the room. I went into a corner and pretended to be examining a painting, a nude by Bonnard, but all the time I was peering around at her. Finally, she stood up, turned on her heel, and marched back through all the rooms, out of the museum, and back to the hotel. I was completely exhausted, not so much by the rapid pace as by my feelings. I scribbled a brief note in the lobby and asked the porter to take it up to Lena's room. Please come to the forest cemetery tomorrow, two p.m. I have a story I want to tell you.

EIGHTEEN

EIGHTEEN

How odd, said Lena, I didn't see you in the museum yesterday. And the rest of the day I didn't notice anyone following me either. I'd have every reason to be furious with you, she said, but I can't manage to blame you for anything, I don't know why. Sometimes it does feel to me as though we'd known each other for a long time. What was it that interested you about those hunting scenes? I asked. I don't know, she said, maybe the feeling of peace they radiate. Quiet after the hunt. Or the quiet after death? I asked. She seemed to think about that. After a while she said, But how can that be? If he's like you, and I'm like your Magdalena, and we're leading the same life as you both, fifteen or twenty years before, then surely our parents would have to be the same and our friends and the buildings we live in, the productions in which Magdalena and I appeared, and the texts that you and Chris write. Then the whole world would be a kind of double

world. And it's not. No, I said, it's not. There are dis-
tinctions, variations. Those are the mistakes, the asym-
metries that make life possible in the first place. I once
talked to a physicist who explained to me that the whole
universe is based on a tiny mistake, a minute imbalance
between matter and antimatter that must have occurred
at the time of the big bang. But for that mistake, matter
and antimatter would long since have canceled one another out, and there would be nothing. Wouldn't any tiny
asymmetry have to multiply, though, asked Lena, any
decision that he or I made differently from you and Magdalena, wouldn't it have to diverge more and more from
your pattern? That's what you'd think, I said, but you
keep returning to the proper way. As though the things
you do had no effect on what actually happens. It's like
having a play put on by several directors. The scenes look
different, even the words can be changed or cut, but the
action follows its unvarying course.

Lena stopped and pulled out her cellphone. I just need
to message Chris, she said, typing out a text. I'm writing to tell him I've gone to the theater. That evening with
those scriptwriters was so deadly. He won't believe you,
I said, he'll be jealous. Is that what happened then? she
asked, putting away her cellphone. We didn't have those
back then. Magdalena wasn't there when I got back to the
hotel. We had had an argument in the morning, and when
she was angry with me, she would often withdraw. Then
she would reappear, as though nothing had happened.

It's true, said Lena, I played Miss Julie, and he helped me learn the part, and that was when we kissed for the first time. I turned to face her. She avoided looking at me, but in spite of the feeble light of the streetlamps, I could see that her face was flushed. It's just occurred to me how much you must know about me if your story is true. I mean... not just where we went on holiday, what we talked about, what happened to us. But really personal, intimate things. The fact that you don't squeeze the toothpaste out of the tube to the end. More personal than that, said Lena.

I didn't say anything, I didn't want to embarrass her further. I was remembering how we had made love the first time, that afternoon. Magdalena was strangely awkward. Her lips were dry, perhaps on account of the fever, and she barely responded to my kisses, though she didn't turn away either. When I pulled off her nightgown, she seemed indifferent, letting it happen as though it was a necessity. After a while, she said, let's go on the bed, it'll be easier.

After that we sometimes made love all night. It wasn't so much about sex, it was more like a kind of unappeasable hunger, a need for proximity, a desire to merge into one another. We lay quite exhausted on the bed, Magdalena propped her head up on her hand and eyed me in bemusement. I drew her closer to me and kissed her, and we began all over again, till at some point one or other of us drifted off.

NINETEEN

NINETEEN

And you had the feeling the whole time there was someone on your tracks? Lena interrupted my thoughts. To
begin with, it drove me crazy, I was furious with him,
maybe I was jealous. But after a while I began to feel
sorry for him. Because he didn't have any choice, the
whole course of his life was set, pre-lived by me. I felt
responsible for him. If everything you do happens twice
over, and each decision you take affects not only you
but someone else as well, who is helpless to do anything
about it, then it's better to think twice before you act.

A strange notion, said Lena, that somewhere there
might be another person like me. Not just someone who
looks like me and is living the same life, but who thinks
and feels like me as well. I think I like the idea. It's like
having a best friend who knows all there is to know about
you and who you know all about, without your needing
to talk about it at all. No, I said, it's as though you're not

a whole person anymore, as though you were dissolving. It's an awful thing. Perhaps everyone has a doppelgänger somewhere, said Lena. You were just unlucky enough to meet yours. I don't know why, I said, but I sometimes have the feeling he only exists on account of me. If I hadn't happened to meet him, he wouldn't exist now. As though he's a child of my memory, a memory that became reality.

Were you never tempted to take a hand in our life together? asked Lena, to correct mistakes you made, to give our life a different turn? Or simply out of curiosity, to see what happens? I'm scared of doing that, I said. Who knows what would happen?

TWENTY

TWENTY

After the second meeting, it took me a while to recover my bearings. I tried not to think about my younger self, but I was addicted to observing him, to check that he really was living my life. And maybe to remember everything too, and experience it all again, though this time as an observer. It wasn't hard to find him, I could look up my old diaries, and wherever I was sixteen years earlier, he would be now. The world had changed, university syllabuses and train timetables were different, he wore different clothes and had a cellphone instead of a landline, but none of it seemed to affect the course of his life particularly.

My book was almost forgotten by now, the invitations were down to a trickle, and my publisher was no longer asking me about the follow-up, because I'd given him too many reassurances. Since I wasn't in any new relationship either, I had endless time. So I followed the man almost incessantly, sat in the lectures he attended, caught up with him outside his house, and followed him on his errands through the city. I shopped where he shopped, drank in bars where he and his friends drank. From time to time our eyes might meet, but it seemed he wasn't aware of it, as though I was invisible or at least of no significance for him.

It felt strange to observe my younger self. I realized how much I had forgotten or misremembered. Often I was dismayed by my younger self's naivety, and it wasn't unusual for me to feel a temptation to give him a jolt, or whisper some good advice in his ear. But I never did, perhaps for fear of the unpredictable consequences of a direct confrontation.

I neglected my work, stopped seeing my friends, no longer went out. Eventually, completely shattered, a nervous wreck, I decided to move to another city, another country. I wanted to be as far from him as possible, so as not to have to see him anymore, and find myself again, and live my own life. After looking for a while, I found a job at a German-language school in Barcelona, a city I had never been to before and where my doppelgänger wouldn't come looking for me. I cleaned up my flat, gave away or sold the bulk of my stuff, and left the rest with friends. And then I went.

I'm hungry, said Lena, and it's getting cold as well. Let's go and eat something. After a while we found a restaurant, a sort of bistro with a small menu. It was rather a gloomy place, with just a few solitary guys sitting there over their beer. Lena chose a table in the middle of the room, it didn't seem to bother her that the other patrons were staring at her. We ordered something and ate in silence. I had a beer, Lena drank water. I need a clear head, she said. What are you doing here, if you don't want to see him again? One thing at a time, I said.

In Barcelona, things picked up. I didn't have much more stuff than would fit into a large suitcase, and I started off living in a cheap pension. I liked working with the children, made friends with the men and women on the staff, and soon found a small apartment in the old town. At first I had a pretty quiet, withdrawn kind of life, it was as though I had to retreat, hide away from myself. Over time, though, I started to move more freely through the little crooked lanes. I sought out places where people congregated, I liked the feeling of being part of a crowd. Sometimes I would drift about half the night, spend hours sitting in cafés, and then after closing time, in clubs, just observing the scene. Near my apartment there was a hotel where lots of Swiss people stayed, and it was fun watching them and listening to them, not suspecting anyone understood their language.

I started a relationship with an Argentine woman, who lived on the floor below me. She was in Spain illegally, and was getting by on various temp jobs. I seemed to think that my life would be harder to pick up, the more uneventful and discreet it was. Via my girlfriend, I met other Argentines, a casual, likable set, all living from hand to mouth, but loyal and helpful whenever one of their number was in trouble with the authorities or with his landlord or employer. Sometime, maybe in my seventh or eighth year, Alma went home. Her father had gotten sick, and she wanted to be with him. We talked about maybe starting a business together in her country, a restaurant or a bookshop or even a Swiss school, but probably we were never that serious about it. I never made it over there to visit her.

Once Alma was gone, I missed her more than I had expected. Even so, we wrote each other less and less. I started thinking about returning to Switzerland. Since I'd been there, Barcelona had gotten more and more touristy, the old town where I was still living was full of backpackers who were only there to drink and hang out together.

Then one Saturday in spring, I saw him. Chris? said Lena. Yes, I said. As I did every Saturday, I'd gone shopping in the Boqueria. And I saw him coming up to me. I recognized him instantly, there was no chance of a mistake. Our eyes met, and this time too he gave no indication of knowing me, he walked past without batting an eyelid. I stopped still in shock, turned around, and set off after him. He strolled through the rows of stalls, not buying anything. I followed him out of the market and then through the old city. He seemed not to have anything in mind, eventually he sat down in a café, bought himself a drink, wrote in a small notebook, and then went on.

I tracked him all day. It was a shock to run into him, and at the same time I felt a vast relief. The fact that he had come here meant that he was leading an autonomous life, that he was doing things I had never done, going to places I had never been to. I began to doubt the whole doppelgänger story. Maybe I was just imagining everything, certainly I had been drunk the very first time we met, and it was all so long ago now that it seemed unreal in my memory, like a bad dream on waking up.

TWENTY-ONE

TWENTY-ONE

I had just paid and the landlord had gone back behind the counter when an old man walked into the bar. He was wearing a thin raincoat and his face was red with cold. He looked around the bar, and seeing us, he took a step in our direction and then stopped as though afraid to come any closer. He said something in German, but so quietly that I had trouble hearing him. It's too late, he said. It will always be too late. He laughed mirthlessly but his eyes swiveled like those of a maniac. After staring into my eyes for a long time, something seemed to swing in him, his stare seemed to fade, and he quickly stalked out of the bar.

Shall we go on? asked Lena, who had been busy with her phone, and seemed not to have noticed the incident. I nodded, and we set off. Chris is bound to be tied up with his dinner till midnight, she said, and I really don't feel like sitting around in the hotel waiting for him. She smiled and put her phone away. Did he reply? I asked. I've never been to Barcelona, said Lena, is it very beautiful? It's warmer than here for a start, I said. The old town is right on the water, there are even sandy beaches. Stockholm is on the water too, said Lena. Or are those just lakes?

While we'd been in the bistro, it had started snowing in little grainy flakes that had formed a thin crust on the roads and pavements, except where pedestrians and cars had left dark traces through it.

The part of town got a little livelier. An open expanse between tenement blocks had been converted to an illuminated ice rink, and people were skating on it. Look at that guy, said Lena, and pointed to a young dark-skinned man who was curving around all by himself, turning pirouettes and even performing the odd leap. He seemed to be dancing for himself, concentrated on himself, slipping in and out among the other skaters as though they didn't exist. Lena stepped out onto the ice. Come on! She took my arm, and we took a few short, cautious steps along the edge of the glittering surface. At the other end of the little park, an old man was roasting chestnuts. We bought a small bag and ate them as we walked on.

TWENTY-TWO

TWENTY-TWO

I don't know what made me decide to tell the whole story to my doppelgänger. Perhaps because it suddenly seemed like an anecdote to me, one of those urban myths that happened to the friend of a friend, and that get passed from one person to the next without anyone actually believing them. When Chris stopped at a light, I walked up beside him, said hello, and asked if he could spare a moment. The sound of his home dialect gave him a turn, but then he said, sure, he wasn't doing anything. I too jumped, not because of the resemblance to my younger self, but because of the differences, which struck me immediately. It was less his appearance than his way of speaking and behaving that had something artificial. Even his general friendliness seemed put on; under the mask of his smile, I saw something pinched and stiff, familiar to me from people who concealed their actual motives but were ruthless in the pursuit of their aims. I couldn't believe that my face had been anything like that sixteen years ago. I took an immediate dislike to him, but it was too late to change my plan.

Chris was just on his way to Barceloneta, an old harbor district on the sea where fishermen and factory workers used to live, but which had in the meantime become as touristy as the old town around the Ramblas. He said he wanted to get to a beach. I'll take you, I said, I know my way around here. I led him along one of the narrow old streets that led through the area in a tight grid. I loved the sea, but I didn't very often come here. When I wanted to go to the beach, I took a train to one of the little towns north of the city, Mataro or Caldetas, where the beaches weren't so crowded, and mainly locals went.

The buildings looked decrepit, most of the ground floor windows were barred. The street was already in shadow, only the second floors of the buildings were still in sun. Some of the balconies had washing hung up to dry on them. The streets were full of a mixture of cooking smells and the briny wind that blew in from the sea, running over our bodies like greedy hands. From the promenade, which was lined with scruffy palms, a flight of steps led down to the beach. There was a cruise ship on the horizon.

As we walked, I told Chris my whole story—our story. Somewhere we sat down in the sand and drank the beers we'd picked up in a little supermarket on the way, and I went on with my story. Behind us, the sun was plunging to the horizon, lengthening our shadows. The high chairs of the lifeguards were deserted, but there were still people in the water, others were playing beach volleyball or simply strolling. It took me a while to realize that the birds looking for food in the sand weren't seagulls but pigeons.

After I'd finished, and Chris had spent a while thinking about what I'd said, he started to ask me questions about our childhood and youth, detailed questions concerning things that no one but ourselves could have known. When I answered correctly, he gave a quick nod, and went on to the next question. If my answer didn't satisfy him, he shook his head, and said, You see! There are deviations, I said, there are bound to be. It's not possible, he said. The story is too crazy, and our conversation has gone on too long for it to be a dream. So, tell me, what's the book going to be called that I'm going to write in a few years' time, the one you say you published a long time ago? I told him the title, and he took out his phone, typed something into it, and said with a malicious smile, There's no such book. Then it's out of print, I said, why wouldn't it be, after so many years? He typed some more. Not available secondhand either, he said, and it's not in the principal library catalogs either. I know the national library ac-quired the book, I said, they buy copies of every book that's published in Switzerland. I went there once with

Magdalena. We ordered it, and she said I ought to sign the copy. A librarian caught me in the act, and she made a gigantic fuss and accused me of vandalizing public property. Maybe the book was withdrawn as a result. Come on, said Chris, you got that out of a film.

TWENTY-THREE

TWENTY-THREE

This is the most painful part of the story, I said. He was right. I must have seen the scene somewhere and made a memory of it, incorporated it into my life. Or Magdalena knew it, and we had performed it in the library. Yes, said Lena, I know the film, it's *Breakfast at Tiffany's*. Could we have seen it together perhaps? I asked. No, she said, shaking her head, I saw it many years ago, I was little more than a girl at the time. Chris performed the search for my book a second time, and showed me what came up on his phone: no results. He laughed in relief. For him this whole thing was a bizarre story that he would tell friends when he got home and make them laugh. But for me it spelled the end of a world, my world, a whole life, the way I remembered it. He went on to Google Magdalena's name and "actor" and found a single entry on the drama school home page. She was called Lena, not Magdalena, he said. Maybe my Magdalena has got married, I suggested, and then changed her name. Maybe she's not acting anymore. You can't find everyone on the Internet. Yes, or maybe your Magdalena never existed, said Chris.

When was this? asked Lena. Four years ago, I said. She counted on her fingers. That was shortly before I met him. The year I passed my final exams at drama school and got my first part.

Chris must have noticed how excited I was, at any rate he stopped asking about our shared past and started concentrating on the years I had on him. Even though he claimed not to believe me, he wanted to hear all about Magdalena, our first meeting, the time we were happy together. Perhaps he was just trying to calm me down by asking about events that I didn't share with him, that were exclusively mine. I was happy to talk, it did me good to have at least some part of my life all to myself, and to be able to assure myself of my memories by telling them to him. I told him how and why Magdalena had left me, and how just a few months afterwards I had written the book, which became the repository for all my grief at our parting. He even wanted to hear the plot of the book, even though this was a book he had just claimed had never existed.

He listened patiently, from time to time he let a handful of sand trickle through his fingers, he gave an occasional nod, and asked a brief question to ascertain a detail or point of chronology. By now the sky had gotten completely dark, but there was still plenty of activity on the beach. There was music playing all around us, and people talking and laughing. When I had got to the end of my story, Chris got up and brushed the sand off his pants. He put his hand out to pull me up, but I didn't take it. I wasn't going to accompany him any farther, having said everything I had to say. It's time I went back to the hotel, he said, I've had hardly anything to eat all day, and I'm tired.

I got up. I was dizzy and might have fallen over if Chris hadn't grabbed me by the shoulder. Are you not well? Should I call a taxi? Suddenly I felt an indescribable fury, I was this close to slapping him. There he was, imagining a quick Internet search was enough to rub out the whole of my life, as though only what was online existed. I shook off his hand and stalked off without another word. When I had climbed the steps up to the promenade, I turned around to look. He was still standing there, head down, apparently lost in thought.

Lena said nothing. She too seemed to be lost in thought. I was silent, I probably couldn't have got it across to her in any case what I felt like after that meeting. The next day I called the school and canceled my classes. I walked around as in a dream and tried to recall my life. That's when I noticed that my memories had changed, that, when I evoked scenes from my own life, I was in Chris's skin, in his world, in his clothes, speaking his words. It felt dimly as though I could remember our Barceloneta meeting, not from my point of view but his.

An older man had told me his life story, and to begin with I had listened in disbelief that turned into the agitation you feel when patterns are crystallized out of life's chaos, and stories emerge. Hadn't this conversation in fact been the beginning of everything?

My fury with Chris kept growing, it was as though he was stealing my life from me by living it himself, blotting it out and thereby blotting me out. Suddenly I was convinced that it would take his death to free me and reinstall me in my rightful place.

I didn't go into school on any of the following days either, instead I walked around looking for Chris. I asked after him in hotels in the old center, but it was hopeless, there had to be hundreds of lodgings. I went around the various sights, to shops that tourists frequented, trotted up and down the Ramblas. All this time, I was making plans for removing Chris without being caught. There was no chance of being suspected, because apart from him and me, no one knew of the secret connection between us. My greatest fear was that he had given me the slip, and already left the city. Astonishingly, all this time I never had the least moral compunction about committing such an act, it was as though he belonged to me, and it was my right to put an end to his life, which was mine. If I had happened to encounter him, God knows what I might have done.

TWENTY-FOUR

TWENTY-FOUR

Lena and I had reached a narrow lake, whose shore was inaccessible behind a wire fence. On the far side of it, made fast to a dock, was a long line of little sailboats. The boats were rocking in the wind, their wires jangled against the masts. We walked along beside the fence on a footpath dimly lit by lanterns. It was a while since either of us had spoken.

I thought of the days of great confusion in Barcelona. If the book didn't exist, what else about my story and my memories could possibly be true? What had my life been? Where had I sprung from? My head reeled, and I was close to going insane. Finally, still without going back to the school, I gave in my notice and packed my case.

After eight years in Barcelona, I was returning to effectively a foreign land. I didn't even try to pick up the threads of my former life. I had run away from it, and now I wanted to start afresh, not see anyone I had known then, and avoid the places where I had spent time. I didn't even call to pick up the belongings I had left with a friend.

On the Internet I had found a tiny furnished sublet, nothing wonderful, but good enough for a beginning. The tenant was an Austrian physics student who was spending a semester abroad. I never met her, when I moved in she was already gone. We communicated by letters and emails, she had left the keys with a neighbor.

The apartment was on the top floor of a Sixties tenement building, the rooms were coolly furnished in pine. On a mattress in a niche there was a clutch of soft toys, by the window was a large desk with a computer. The bookshelf contained a few textbooks and computer manuals, nothing else. In the kitchen was a bulletin board with sayings and Bible verses and snapshots. Most of the photos had been taken outdoors, laughing women in meadows, throwing their arms around each other's shoulders. They were wearing jeans, and tracksuits, bathing suits in one of the pictures. A few of the faces were represented several times, none of them was in any way remarkable. I wondered which one of them was the tenant, or perhaps she was the one who had taken the pictures. She had written to tell me she was leaving all her things in the apartment and I was to make myself at home. But for all the snapshots and the cuddly toys, the rooms felt somehow deserted, as though no one had been there for months. Maybe that's why I felt so much at home there now, as my life was an empty space, with only the occasional shadow on the walls to indicate that it had once been lived in.

It was the beginning of summer, and I sent out a few halfhearted applications to high schools. I wasn't surprised that other applicants were preferred. At the employment agency I was advised to look for supply jobs, and after some more time looking, I finally got a short-term job filling in at a boarding school in Engadin, not far from the place I'd first met Magdalena.

My memories of that first summer of my return are a blur. I didn't do much; even when the weather was fine I stayed in the small apartment; it took me a long time to recover myself. The more I thought about the story, the more convinced I was that it wasn't me who had been mistaken but Chris, and that he was, possibly maliciously, concealing from me the traces of my life with Magdalena. I didn't need evidence for a life I had lived and could remember. Even so, I didn't embark on any further research, perhaps I was secretly afraid Chris might be right after all and that my whole life might be a lie, a figment. I preferred to think back to the time Magdalena and I had gotten to know each other, had gone up into the mountains together, had playful conversations, how I used to go and pick her up from the theater, how we kissed for the first time, and slept together. In my mind I was reliving the beginning of our relationship, and my yearning for Magdalena was as strong as it had been when she left me. Without any particular plan, I sat down one night and wrote out the first sentence of the book I had written sixteen years before, and that Chris claimed didn't exist. By all means, let Chris meet his Lena, and fall in love with her and be loved by her, he would never be able to take my Magdalena and my book away from me.

TWENTY-FIVE

TWENTY-FIVE

The path had left the lakeside and led through a thin copse of trees. After a couple of hundred yards, we were back beside the water. Apart from us, there was no one around, and the sounds of the city were only dimly audible. Lena spoke first. Do you remember, she asked in a quiet and very soft tone, how we went to France three years ago? Nineteen years, I said, yes, how could I not. We had borrowed a car from friends and just set out without any particular plan or destination. Those were our best holidays, said Lena, I've never felt as unencumbered as that either before or since. We didn't even have a map, there was no place we were going to, so it was impossible for us to get lost. We drove across country, avoided the bigger towns, and ended up in sleepy villages that looked as though nothing had happened in them for decades. We took recommendations for hotels and restaurants from locals, spent a day or two in a place, and drove on. It's a huge country, said Lena. That was how we first got to know each other.

I was surprised to hear her say that. At the time I was very much in love with Magdalena, but it was during those very holidays that I became aware of how alien she was to me. Sometimes, when I looked at her, I had the feeling I had never seen her before. I see an unmade bed, I said, and Magdalena in her underwear in front of the mirror, looking at herself. There's a knock. Will you open? she asked. I'm not wearing anything and call out to the maid to just leave breakfast outside. When she's gone, I bring the tray in and set it down on the bed. Croissants and little plastic cups of butter labeled LE PRÉSIDENT, and apricot jam and milky coffee that tastes bitter and burnt. Magdalena sits down cross-legged on the bed opposite me. She smiles at me and I lean forward across the tray and kiss her.

You see, said Lena, and no one can take that away from you. She had stopped still and was facing me. We stood very close looking at each other, in the feeble light her eyes looked black and opaque. Then she kissed me on the mouth, just quickly, it felt like the memory of a kiss. Before I could say anything, she had turned away and walked on.

TWENTY-SIX

I had thought I had my novel in my head word for word and scene for scene, but when I started writing it out again, the memory dissolved, and I realized how much I had forgotten. It was like a dream, where everything seems to be perfectly clear, but which recedes at once, the moment you try and look at it hard, concentrate on it. My recollection of the book didn't consist of words and sentences, but feelings, which are much more precise than any thought could ever be, but at the same time elusive.

The book I wrote at that time wasn't really the story of Magdalena and me. After she had suggested I might write about her, I soon realized I wouldn't be able to do that, that I was too compromised to see her or write about her clearly. The fictive Magdalena had covered the real one, as a mask covers a face. That was the subject of my book, the images we have of one another, and the power these images have over us.

I remembered the Stockholm workshop, where the American script doctor had told us how to construct a scene, tell a story, write a screenplay, that would hack it on the market. I sensed at the time that living texts could never be written this way, texts that had anything to do with me and the things I was interested in. I saw my career ahead of me as a TV writer who wrote exactly those technically flawless screenplays that the stations wanted, who kept regular hours and had no financial worries. I would write Magdalena the parts she wanted, no deathless scenes, just entertainment fodder for which the market was much greater than it was for literature. Life is good, people are kind, and any conflict can be resolved by the end of the episode, or at the very latest the end of the series. And so we lived. We led a good, pain-free life, lived in a tastefully decorated apartment, were popular attendees at premieres and openings. We were recognized on the street, the successful actress and her writer husband, a perfect couple.

We were sitting at a long table in a smart restaurant in the inner city, everyone was talking and laughing together. Next to me the director was talking to me about one of my characters and whom he could imagine playing the part. I had meant to suggest Magdalena, but I couldn't do it, it was bad enough that I had written such crap, I really didn't want her playing it.

Dinner was a long time in coming, and in spite of the prices, we had drunk a fair amount of wine already. We'll put it on the bill for dinner, said the director, laughing. He had ordered elk steak, but when the food came, he pushed his plate away after the very first bite and summoned the waiter. I wanted my meat *saignant*, he said furiously, do you call this *saignant*? He jabbed his fork into the meat and waved it under the waiter's nose. Do you even know what *saignant* means? Bloody, red, got it? He dropped the meat on the plate and told the waiter to take it back. With the prices you charge, you can surely expect the cook knows how to fry a steak to order. The scene seemed to embarrass the waiter, who apologized in quiet tones and took the plate back. The director went on speaking to me, as though nothing had happened, but I no longer heard him. I got up and left.

It took me a long time to find the hotel. We had gone to the restaurant in a group, and I hadn't paid any attention to the way. But I didn't want to take a taxi, I needed fresh air and time to reflect. By the time I found the hotel and walked into our room, Magdalena wasn't there.

I didn't ask myself later whether the decision that night in Stockholm had been the right one or not. It was one of those decisions after which you can't imagine an alternative. To go was the only possibility, to keep going on, without stopping, and without knowing where to.

TWENTY-SEVEN

The summer vacation was over, and I turned up for my new job in the Engadin. The boarding school had something of the atmosphere of a sanatorium, a secluded world far away from everything else. I was given a small furnished attic apartment in a building where the janitor had once used to live, and that was now given over to temporary teaching staff.

The pupils seemed to like me, I didn't make any very great demands of them and gave them better grades than my predecessor had done. On my days off I went for hikes in the vicinity and worked on the revised version of my novel. I wasn't in any particular hurry, I was writing it out in longhand, to slow the process down, and to get a sense of every word. Time in the book passed barely any faster than it did in real life. As I wrote, all my feelings came back to me, my love for Magdalena, the mingled sense of alienation and proximity when we were together, my fear of losing her, and then my grief at the loss. Sometimes I would lose myself in daydreaming, sit there for hours in my little attic, look out of the window at the landscape which, even before my eyes, merged into the scenes of my recollection. There were things now that I had a superior understanding of, things Magdalena had said or done, and I could see how difficult I had made things for her. With youthful pathos, I had believed I had to decide between her and my writing, between freedom and love. Only now did I understand that love and freedom were not mutually exclusive, but mutually entailed: the one wasn't possible without the other.

I had intended to write the exact same book again, but while I was working on it, it turned imperceptibly into a different one. I groped forward through a world that created itself before my eyes, found different routes, saw and heard my characters say and do different things, and situations that had originally seemed intractable to me suddenly seemed to offer ways out of them.

TWENTY-EIGHT

TWENTY-EIGHT

It was the end of September, a cool, sunny day. I had the afternoon off, after lunch most of the pupils took off on the train to St. Moritz or God knows where. I went on one of my usual long walks, taking the same paths as always. I wasn't interested in variety, I was happy to have each day like the one before. Sometimes Magdalena took my hand, but she never stayed by my side for long. She would stoop to pick up a blade of grass or walk backwards in front of me, teeter along fallen tree trunks when we were in a forest, or point out a leaf that was caught in an invisible spider's thread and seemed to be hanging in midair. She seemed barely any older than when we'd first met, many years ago.

Do you know those moments in autumn, when you suddenly think it's spring? I asked, as we emerged from the forest. I don't know what causes it, a smell or bird song, the low position of the sun. It's a feeling of transitoriness that suddenly emerges, and as suddenly disappears.

On a bench at the edge of the forest were a boy and girl from my class, sitting close and holding hands. They greeted me sheepishly, barely raising their eyes to look at me. Even though they were doing nothing forbidden, it suddenly seemed embarrassing to be seen by me. I had stopped, wanting to say something to them, warn them of mistakes I had made at their age, encourage them or simply wish them good luck and say how nice it was to see them sitting there like that. In the end I only smiled at them and wished them a good afternoon. Only when I moved on did I notice that Magdalena had disappeared.

TWENTY-NINE

TWENTY-NINE

We were walking along the side of a six-lane highway, with a board fence and an enormous building site behind it. A cold wind blew in our faces, but Lena didn't complain, she walked along at my side as though she had never done anything else. Finally, we got to a brightly lit crossing, with a gas station on it, and on the other side an entrance to the university campus. The university buildings were soulless and modern, but the warm light at the windows seemed to radiate security. Shall we warm up in there? asked Lena, as we passed in front of a student dorm. Not here, I said, and led her around the complex of buildings. There was a constant roar of traffic from the highway. The campus lawns had more snow on them than other parts of the city, but the footpaths had been swept clean.

Do you know your way around here then? asked Lena. Sure, I replied, I was here once a long time ago.

With me? she asked. No, I said, holding open the door to the library for her.

The entrance was deserted, only at the information center was an employee sitting, twiddling around with his phone. We walked up a wide flight of stairs. There was an open section with long wooden shelves and tables. On the walls were signs enjoining the patrons to silence. Not many seats were occupied. None of the patrons had a book in front of them, they all were working on laptops, some of them with headphones, their expressions were closed off, as though their consciousnesses were somewhere else. When I was a student, I said, we used to go to the library to get acquainted. Our eyes met, and we went to the cafeteria or met outside the door for a smoke.

We walked through the densely clustered stacks. The books were arranged following some inscrutable system. Lena pulled a thick volume off one of the shelves and flicked through the pages, it was a rather tattered copy of an anthology of English poetry. Did you ever write poems? she asked me. Someone once said prose writers write about the world, poets write about themselves, I said. Do you think that's true? asked Lena. I shrugged. Maybe the opposite's just as true.

I took the volume from her and looked for a Robert Frost poem in the index that I wanted to read her, but when I found it, I saw another, that seemed still more apposite to me. I read the first few lines to myself. When

I looked up to show Lena the poem, she had already moved on, and I returned the book to the shelf.

Lena walked along ahead of me, I couldn't see her face, only heard her halting voice. Did it ever occur to you that it might all be your imagination? I've long since stopped asking myself that, I said. I don't think I'm crazy, but if I were, how would I know it? I do what I have to do. I'd like to believe you, she said. I don't want to know what the future has in store for me, but I like the idea that it's already written down, and that everything that happens to me has happened to someone else and fits in a pattern and makes sense. As though my life were a story. I think that's what I always liked about books. The fact that you can't change them. You don't even have to read them. It's enough to own them, and pick them up, and know that they will always remain the way they are. She sat down at one of the desks and I sat down diagonally across from her. What time is it? she asked. I think the library's closing soon, I said, getting up. Of course I've doubted myself. This whole story drives me crazy. But what should I do? Presumably it was the doubting it that caused me not to let the thing alone. In Barcelona I told Chris so much about Magdalena that it would be a simple matter for him to find you. If he really is my doppelgänger, there is nothing I can do to stop him. But if everything is purely imagination, then I played you into his hands the moment I told him your name. That makes me responsible for what will happen.

THIRTY

THIRTY

I had read a newspaper review of the play with the fish. The reviewer was underwhelmed, but Lena was singled out as a highly promising newcomer. There was an accompanying photograph of her in one scene, indistinct but unmistakable. The photo brought out all my feelings of the time, and much more powerfully than if I had just been thinking of Magdalena. It was like having her in my hands. I clipped it carefully and pinned it to my fridge with a magnet.

Weeks and months went by, and I thought about going to pick Magdalena up at the stage door, and wandering about with her half the night and talking, with the sole aim of stopping time and not having to go to sleep yet. Then came the day we had first made love. Even as I was getting up, I had to think that Lena would soon call Chris and tell him she was ill, and did he want to come and visit her. That day I wasn't good for anything.

I couldn't concentrate, and the pupils monkeyed around till I shouted at them so loud that one of them stayed behind at the end of class and asked me in worried tones if I was all right.

Weeks later, I saw the ad for *Miss Julie*, the play Magdalena was having her breakthrough in, put on by a young female director I hadn't heard of. I dawdled, let the premiere go by, then one day I booked a ticket, got a room for the night, and on Friday after the end of classes traveled down from the mountains to see the play.

I could barely remember the production sixteen years ago. I had only had eyes for Magdalena then, and remembered how jealous I felt of the actor playing Jean. Magdalena and I had even fought about him, because she claimed it wasn't her kissing the actor, but Julie kissing Jean, and I called that sophistical nonsense.

The new production was an overwrought farrago of various concepts, to begin with the actors appeared in historical costume, later on they stood around the stage in skimpy leather bondage gear. The relationship between Julie and Jean was depicted as a sadomasochistic power struggle; to crashing rock chords Julie hurt herself and let herself be handcuffed by Jean, only later to become a dominatrix and make him her toy and humiliate him. Somewhere I gave up trying to follow the crazy action and wasn't even attending to the words anymore. I only saw Lena, who was self-assured and confident throughout, retaining her dignity even as she knelt down in front of Jean and unzipped his pants. I was astonished by her talent and force, which in the time I was in love with her had somehow escaped me. Suddenly she seemed very different from the Magdalena in my recollection, and I understood that she was completely independent, and needed neither me nor anyone else.

I hadn't noticed Chris in the theater, but when I was waiting by the stage door after the show, he suddenly appeared. He seemed nervous, chain-smoking, and dropped his cigarette on the pavement the instant Lena appeared. They kissed in the casual way of an established couple, exchanged a few words, and set off.

I followed them at a distance up the hill through ever emptier precincts. Perhaps I was still under the impression of the play, but I had the sense of Lena leading Chris on a chain, like a dog. She always seemed to be a step ahead of him, and his posture had something eager, almost craven, about it.

They headed for the zoo, and then made west along the wooded ridge at the top. From there you could have a splendid view across the city and the lake, but the two were so engrossed in their conversation that they seemed not even to be aware of it. I recalled a line I'd read somewhere about there being nothing more lonely than a pair of lovers. I looked down at the city and tried to remember what we'd spoken about back in the day. But when I turned back to the bench, Lena and Chris were gone.

Some distance away, at the edge of the woods, was an old inn that had a tour bus parked in front of it. Next to the entrance stood a couple of men in dark suits smoking cigarettes. They seemed drunk, were talking at the same time, and kept bursting out laughing. I peered through a window, but the room I found myself looking into wasn't the public bar but a small side room where a wedding group was celebrating, a colorful confusion of festively clad men and women. Their meal had been taken away, now the tables were littered with empty bottles and glasses and crumpled napkins. On a cart were the remnants of a gigantic wedding cake. The bridal couple sat alone at a table facing the window. It took me a second look to see who they were. It was Lena and Chris. They looked totally different from a moment ago. Lena had her hair pinned up in a complicated coiffure and was wearing white, Chris was in black tails. They both seemed tired and out of sorts.

The guests had formed up into little groups, some of them standing, others seated at the various tables. They were leaning in, presumably to hear each other better in spite of the loud music that I could hear outside, a medley of old pop tunes. It was played by a lean man of sixty or so in a glittering purple jacket, whose face looked familiar to me. In fact, a lot of these faces looked familiar to me, and suddenly it dawned on me that these guests were actors whom I had seen that evening onstage and in the lobby, and some of whom had been in the troupe back in Magdalena's day. I had had a conversation during the intermission with Ulrich, the man on keyboard, we had talked about old times, now I barely recognized him. No one was listening to the music and no one was dancing, but that didn't seem to bother him. With a devilish grin on his face he was pounding on the keys as though accompanying a silent film, a burlesque comedy of mixed identities, in which Lena was playing the lead role. At that moment there was a guffaw from the smokers outside. I turned around but couldn't see them from where I was standing. When the laughter died down, I looked into the room again. The lights had been turned out, and there was no one to be seen. The dirty plates and glasses were still on the tables.

THIRTY-ONE

If it was up to me, I don't think I would have had a reception, said Lena, it was all so hurried, but Chris insisted he wanted a proper wedding with all the trimmings, as though our vows wouldn't have meant anything without. That morning we'd been in church, me all in white, him in his dark suit. We even paid for a photographer, who took pictures of us down by the lake. We spent the afternoon on a steamship on the lake, and then a yellow postbus with flowers on the hood took us to the reception. There was roast pork with mashed potatoes and a three-tier wedding cake with a marzipan bride and groom on top. Lots of our friends from the theater were there, there were long, emotional speeches, indiscretions, a director who by afternoon had had too much to drink and was telling off-color jokes, the whole wretchedness of a middle-class wedding. Everything came to an end in a drunken chaos. Chris and I got into an argument, I can't remember why, and by the time we were finally home, and he was carrying me across the threshold, he was so clumsy about it he hit my head against the doorframe and gave me a bump. So much for the happiest day of my life.

That can't be, I said, I never married Magdalena. It never occurred to us. There are deviations, Lena said softly, so softly I wasn't sure if it was sorrow in her voice or merriment.

We were sitting at a small table in the library hall, drinking thin machine coffee. It was madness, Lena was saying, when Chris asked me to be his wife we had barely been together for a month. I was completely unprepared for it. And it probably sounds funny, but I had the sense he wasn't sure about it either, as if he had the idea from someone else.

I was completely confused and wondered what difference Chris and Lena's wedding made to anything. He's on his way here, I finally ended up saying. He decided in favor of writing, proper writing, and he's run away from the workshop and his secure existence as a hack. Now he's blundering around the city just as we are now, just as I did then.

THIRTY-TWO

Back in the hotel, I racked my brains over what I was going to tell Magdalena; how I was going to break it to her that her nice dream of our twin careers in TV was over, that I would rather stack shelves in a supermarket than write texts I despised. That morning already we'd had a quarrel when I had poked fun at the American and those American films that always offered an audience what it expected and wanted. I had been puzzled how passionately Magdalena had stood up for films she hadn't in some cases even seen; I couldn't shake the suspicion that what was at issue between us was more than a few mediocre Hollywood productions. Even now I wasn't sure whether what I was running away from was being a TV wage slave or Magdalena and her notion of a happy and fulfilled life.

I could no longer bear to wait for her. The hotel room felt like a prison, I needed to get out, walk around, breathe the air, and think.

It was dark outside. The shops were still open, it was the sale season, and lots of people were out and about, their hands full of shopping bags and parcels. I avoided the big, lit-up avenues, and after a while found myself wandering through residential streets, deserted commercial districts, large shopping centers, anonymous office blocks, factories, and warehouses. All I had on was a thin raincoat, and I felt hungry and cold. There were no restaurants where I was, but on a corner I saw a pub with a selection of bar food.

It was gloomy in there. A few of the tables were occupied by men on their own, drinking beer and staring into space. I ordered a beer and something to eat. As I was eating, I was forcibly reminded of the early days with Magdalena, that now, in retrospect, struck me as the happiest time of my life. At some point we must have mislaid our happiness, I couldn't say how or when it had come about. I had decided on a different path for myself. The notion of middle-class contentment that Magdalena had devised for us was not mine, and in my story, there was, to be brutally honest, no room for her.

After I'd eaten and warmed up a little, I set out again, walked on, and found myself in more welcoming areas. Between tenement buildings there was an ice rink that was lit up by powerful lights on poles, a white square, cut out of the dark world by dazzling brightness. For a while I stood and watched the skaters slide effortlessly over the surface and trace their circles. I could still have gone back, Magdalena surely wasn't expecting me before midnight. But I walked on. My agitation eased a little, and at the same time my certainty grew that there was no way back. It was too late, too late to be happy.

I had no idea where I was going, even so I felt somehow liberated. I got to a lake, and then a broad landscaped expanse full of large buildings. One entrance was lit up, and when I approached, I saw that it was the university library. There was almost no one inside. I walked up to the top floor, where there were a few chairs and tables and cubicles, pulled a book off the shelf at random, and sat down at one of the tables, which were partitioned in the middle. Facing me was a woman, neither young nor especially striking-looking, with a stack of books and notebooks. I browsed in my book, a Norton poetry anthology, and read some of the poems in it. After some time, the woman asked me a question in Swedish. I replied in English that I didn't understand. The time, she said, now in English, tapping her wrist with a finger. I forgot my watch. Damn, she said, when I told her, they're about to close. Would you happen to know if there's a hotel anywhere near? I asked. I don't think so, she said, there's no shortage of student accommodation, but you can't get into that unless you're registered with the university, and there's a long waiting list. Are you a student? No, I said, I'm just looking for somewhere to stay the night. You're leaving it a bit late, she said, laughing. I asked if she was a student. She said she was a postgraduate. I'm working at the Karolinska Institut, across the lake from here. There's a Best Western there, I think. She said her name was Elsa. Something was announced over the public-address system. They're closing, said Elsa, we'd better go. She packed her things, and we headed for the exit together. Outside, I lit a cigarette, and she asked me for one. I've given up, she said, it's not something you do if you're a med student, but when there's one going . . . She asked me what I was doing in Stockholm. It's complicated, I said. As we set off, I told her I was attending a screenwriters' workshop. I didn't say anything about Magdalena. And they didn't book a hotel for you? asked Elsa. No, they did, I said, but I ran away. I don't feel like writing to order. Skipping school then, she said, *tsk, tsk.* And now you're scared to go back, because you think you'll be punished. Something like that, I said. Do you feel like a drink? There's a bar called the Professorn, she said, that's just five minutes from here. They don't shut till one.

It did me good to talk to Elsa. She laughed and joked a lot. She had grown up in a mining town way up in the north called Kiruna. Her father and mother had both worked in the mines. She was a year older than me. I put in a few detours, she said, but it's a long way from Kiruna to here.

The Professorn was a pretty funky bar, where you could order pizza and kebab. It was situated in a large complex of student accommodations just north of the actual campus. A couple of thousand students live there, said Elsa, myself included.

You don't need to tell me the rest, said Lena, getting up, I can perfectly well imagine it. She headed quickly for the way out. When I caught up to her, she suddenly stopped and looked at me with shining eyes. I thought she was about to start crying. He's almost finished the book, she said. That can't be, I said. I didn't marry Magdalena, and I only wrote the book later, after we split up. He can't write it yet because he hasn't felt what I felt then, the pain at our breakup, the loss, the solitude. Your pain can't have been that great if you hop into bed with the first Swede you meet, said Lena furiously. I never slept with her, I said. It's true, she invited me back, but nothing happened.

THIRTY-THREE

THIRTY-THREE

After the third or fourth round of drinks, Elsa did indeed offer to put me up. You don't look like a maniac, she said, why not, I've got enough room.

I tried to explain it to Magdalena the next morning. When I walked into our room, I found her lying on the bed, completely dressed. She looked exhausted and puffy from crying. In a dull voice, she asked me where I'd been all night, but when I started to tell her, she interrupted me to say how she'd got back to the hotel a little before midnight, and had seen the editor and the director down at the bar. They had told her I'd run out of the restaurant, they couldn't say where to or why. When Magdalena didn't find me up in the room, she had gone back downstairs, but by now they'd closed the bar, and there was no one around. She hadn't slept a wink all night, had stayed up waiting for me, worried about me. I just needed to get away, I said, I'm sorry, I was drunk. That's not the point, said Magdalena, crying. You should just admit you don't want to be with me anymore. Or has your courage deserted you already? I don't know what's more contemptible. She watched in silence as I packed my suitcase. I hesitated briefly in the doorway, but, not knowing what to say, I left without any further words of explanation or goodbye. I spent the next two nights in a room in a cheap pension. I saw Magdalena for the last time at the airport.

THIRTY-FOUR

I didn't cheat on Magdalena, I said again. What difference does it make? said Lena. I thought, if you and Chris met up here, everything could turn out differently, I said. He would come to his senses, you would have your conversation, go back to the hotel together, everything would turn out for the best. And he wouldn't write his novel, said Lena. That's what you're about, isn't it? Her voice still sounded angry. I think we're capable of resolving our differences ourselves. Or do you think you can sort out your own life by interfering in ours? The past is past, I said. The question is, are you prepared to allow him a better life, said Lena, or do you want to wreck it just like you wrecked your own? I didn't wreck my life, I said, I decided in favor of literature, and made certain sacrifices. Well? said Lena, and was it worth it?

There was an announcement on the p.a., and a few young people with rucksacks and cases filed past us and out into the night. I watched them go, perhaps I was expecting to see Elsa, but I didn't think she would recognize me after such a long time. Chris won't come, said Lena. He's got no reason to run away. He's found a publisher for his book, it's coming out next spring. You told him the story. I read a draft, it's a good plot.

I had been intending to show Lena my manuscript, had brought it with me to let her see it, and leave its fate in her hands. But my rucksack was gone. I must have left it in the bar. The blood shot to my face, and I felt faint. How does he end his story? I asked. It's a happy ending, said Lena. The woman gets pregnant, she loses the baby, but the loss brings the two of them together. In the end, they decide to move away and begin a new life somewhere else.

I had to laugh, a mean, ugly laugh. How can he know? I asked. How can he know it'll end well? The story I told him doesn't have a good ending. Lena smiled sympathetically. In that case, he changed it. I think his editor may have suggested it. You can't change an ending just like that, I said. The publisher thinks the novel will be a big hit, said Lena. Yes, I said, could well be.

A man in uniform came up to us, and said—in English, as though he'd immediately known we were foreigners—we had to leave, the library was closing. Lena's phone had been ringing for a while now, and she took it out of her pocket, looked at the display, and put it away again. He says the dinner's over now, and he's on his way back to the hotel. Don't you want to write back? I asked. She dismissed my question with a gesture. You've taken advantage of me, both of you in your different ways, she said. Her voice didn't sound livid anymore, just tired. Perhaps he more than you, he did everything right and thus everything wrong.

THIRTY-FIVE

While we'd been in the library, the skies had cleared, and it was even colder than before. Where shall we go? I asked. You must have a copy of your manuscript at home, said Lena. I shook my head. No, I was writing it by hand. Then you must go back to the bar and find it, she said. I'm sure it's still there. Who would steal a manuscript? What about you? I asked. She said she was going on, she hated to retrace her steps. So do I, I said, let's go on together.

The lights inside the building went out, and it took a while for my eyes to get used to the illumination of the lamps along the paths. Look at the stars, said Lena, pointing. Do you know the constellations? Only the Big Dipper, I said, and I can't see it anywhere. There's Orion, she said, and right next to it are the twins Castor and Pollux. Do you know the story? One was divine, the other mortal, and yet they were inseparable.

After a short pause, she said she and Chris had had a fight this morning. The dinner yesterday made me think. I told him he should leave the workshop. I don't like the people, and I don't like what they do to him. She laughed. I said pretty much what you said to your Magdalena that time. I'd rather be a cashier in a supermarket than play a part in one of these series. He worked out how much he stood to earn if a project took off. He could still write other, serious things on the side, he reckoned. Only he wouldn't earn much money for them. But we're doing all right, I said, we've enough to live on, and we do what we want and what we enjoy. It's not worth selling your soul for some extra cash. They don't want my soul, he said, and it's a pile of cash. He went back to doing his sums, worked out the royalties for a second and a third series, speculated on repeats and syndications with other stations. We could retire on it, he said. At that, I left. I was off in the city when I turned up your message, which the porter had given me the night before, and which I'd stuffed in my handbag. I don't know if I'd have taken you up on your invitation if Chris and I hadn't had a fight. And are you sorry you came? I asked. I don't think so, she said.

We wandered around the park on winding paths, but we didn't care, we weren't going anywhere, we didn't even have a direction to go in. I had suggested looking for the Professorn, the pub I had been in sixteen years before with Elsa, but Lena didn't want to. He'd probably show up there, she said, and just at the moment he's the last person I'd like to run into. She said in the past months she had often felt alone when she was with Chris, in fact ever since their wedding she had had the sense of living with a stranger. Maybe a good ending is even harder for me than a bad one.

She asked me how my story ended. In the book I was writing then, the woman leaves and doesn't come back. The story ends shortly after her departure. After that, everything is possible. No, said Lena, not everything. I can't go back to him. I'm not even angry with him, but he's even stranger to me than he was before we met. Did you write something about him in your diary? I asked. Yes, she said, nothing earth-shattering. Only that I'd met a nice man and had gone hiking with him, and that he had tried something on. At that time, I was in love with the author of the play, who was with us in the mountains. Only he was married and much older than me, it would never have worked out. Who knows, I said. Lena shook her head. I think the only reason I went hiking with Chris was to make that guy jealous. Was he in love with you then, the playwright? I asked. Lena shrugged. That's another story.

We had left the campus, and were now walking along the highway, past the dark premises of the Museum of Natural History. I was in there the day before yesterday, said Lena, they've got an exhibition of Swedish fauna, with adorable old-fashioned dioramas with stuffed elks

and reindeer and wolves. You do like your dead animals,
I said. Funny, I never thought about that, said Lena.
Maybe you're right. There's something very dependable
about them. Plus, they don't bite.

Our way led through a rather unbuilt-up area, and
I was thinking we had left the city behind, when we
crossed a bridge and walked into a residential neighborhood. We followed the bank to a second, narrower
bridge. Only once we had crossed it did we realize that
we were on a small wooded island.

You could have found a good ending for your book,
said Lena, don't you think most stories end well? It's not
up to me, I said, writing is more to do with what you
find than what you make. You never know what you'll
find in advance. When I was writing the book for the
second time, I discovered something different than the
first time, a different set of possibilities. I'm not sure if
it's improved the story, but that's not the point.

At the far end of the island was a restaurant, a white-
washed wooden building with a terrace that looked like
a simple family dwelling. There were lights on, and
through the window we could see a group of people in
formal dress. A man in a dark suit seemed to be giving a
speech. Look, said Lena, pointing to a corner where there
stood a three-tiered wedding cake with a little bridal couple on top. The beginning of a new story.

We walked down to the water, where there was a
pier. We leaned against a railing and looked across to the

lights on the opposite shore. We were silent for a while, then I asked, Do you recognize something of him in me? I didn't know what answer would come or what I even hoped to hear. Lena thought for a long time, then she said: You're both too similar and too different. If I knew for a fact, if I was certain that he would one day be like you, then I could probably go back to him. But maybe the only way he would become like you is if I leave him, if his life is wrecked, the way yours was.

She asked if I saw anything of my Magdalena in her. Everything, I said, you are just exactly what she was, your movements, your laugh, your lightness, your seriousness. Did you never try to find out what happened to her? asked Lena. No, I said. But then I found out by accident. It was that evening I saw you act for the first time. When I was playing Miss Julie? Yes, I said. During the intermission I ran into a former colleague of Magdalena's. Ulrich? asked Lena. Yes, I said. The man who played keyboard at her wedding. He recognized me, and we talked about old times for a bit, and he said he had run into Magdalena recently, and she was married and living in Engadin. She seemed content, thought Ulrich, and she was just as good-looking as she was before.

There are variations, said Lena. Yes, I said, but in the end, everything happens the way it must. And that would be the happy end? she asked. I don't know, I said. In reality there is no ending, only death. And that's rarely happy. Once Magdalena and I thought about how we'd like to die. I argued for freezing to death, maybe because they say that's a good way to go. But Magdalena didn't agree with that, she said she hated feeling cold. She would rather die in the bath with a glass of wine and some music. And of course not before she was good and old. I tried to imagine her as an old woman and myself as an old man and was surprised that the idea didn't scare me, on the contrary it seemed attractive, as though from the beginning that had been the destination for our love. A house, they say, is only finished when it's turned into a ruin.

Your Magdalena seems like a very sensible woman, said Lena. I had followed her up to the restaurant. We're on an island, she said, and if we're not to freeze to death we've no option but to go back the same way. I'm going to call us a taxi.

We stepped into the restaurant. While Lena was talking to a waiter, I looked into the private room, where they were celebrating the wedding. There was a musician playing on a keyboard, and people were dancing. Lena came up alongside me. The taxi'll be here in a couple of minutes, she said, it'll wait for us on the bridge. Aren't weddings depressing? I asked. That depends on who you're marrying, said Lena.

In the taxi she asked the driver to take us to the Best Western. As we were driving there, she was typing on her phone. When we arrived, I got out with her and followed her into the hotel. Just before the reception desk, she turned to me and said: I'm not playing anymore now. It's very simple. I'm going to take a room, and tomorrow I'll see if I can rebook the return flight. She asked the night porter for a single room. I heard him quote her the price, and tell her how to get there, and ask her if she needed the code for the Internet. No, said Lena, laughing, all I need now is a warm bed. With the key card in her hand, she walked back to me. That was an instructive afternoon, she said, I'm not sure whether I should thank you for it or not. She said she wished me all the luck. I do too, I said. Shall we exchange phone numbers? I don't think so, said Lena. No offense, but I think it's better if we don't have any more contact. Who knows, I said, maybe fate has other ideas. Who knows, said Lena, and let me kiss her on the cheek.

THIRTY-SIX

THIRTY-SIX

The taxi was still waiting in front of the hotel when I stepped outside. The driver looked at me expectantly. I shook my head and walked off in the direction of the city. I wondered if I should look for the bar where I'd forgotten my rucksack, but I doubted whether I'd be able to find the place, I didn't even feel convinced that it actually existed.

I passed the city library and entered a park, a wooded hill. It was as though I was entering another world. On top of the hill was an old observatory that no longer seemed to be in use. I looked up at the sky, recognized Orion and the Twins, which Lena had shown me a while earlier. And now I could see the Big Dipper as well. The wind up here was stronger than down in the streets, and the roaring in my ears drowned the sounds of the city. I leaned against a tree and ran my ice-cold fingertips over its rough bark. I had to think of the night I'd seen

Lena as Miss Julie. Ulrich, her colleague, had come up to me during the intermission as though expecting me. He asked me how I liked the production. I'm not really sure, I said, it does take a few liberties. He giggled and said, did you know, at the end it's not Miss Julie who dies, but Jean. That's what you get when you let a woman direct. But the girl's good in the part. I asked him if he could remember the old production, sixteen years ago. The two actresses are just like each other, I said. Don't you think? He thought about it briefly, and shook his head. He told me he had seen Magdalena again not long ago. She invited us all to her wedding, he said, all the old gang. It was great fun. And who did she marry? I asked. The young man she met when she was hiking in the mountains, do you remember? He went hiking with her, and later he would always pick her up after the show. They were together for a while, then they broke up, and years later met up again. Almost like a novel. And how have you been? I shrugged. That's another story.

THIRTY-SEVEN

THIRTY-SEVEN

It's odd, there are years in my life of which I remember practically nothing, they seemed to have passed without a trace. Even major events that changed my life, real turning points, I often don't remember them, it's as though they had taken place without any help from me, in my absence. And then again there are little scenes, on the face of it completely insignificant, and twenty or thirty years later they're as vivid to me as though they had only just happened.

It's a chilly Sunday morning between Christmas and New Year's. I'm not yet twenty, and living with my parents. I've woken up early, and can't get back to sleep. The house is perfectly quiet. A few days ago it snowed, and the snow is still lying there. I decide to take a walk.

Even though the sky is clouded over, the air is terribly clear. The snow muffles the sounds, and if thin ribbons of smoke weren't issuing from the chimneys, you might think the world was utterly depopulated. I leave the village in the direction of the river, where a suspension bridge for pedestrians and cyclists leads to the next village. I have almost crossed the bridge when I notice a body lying there, on the other side, where the path starts to climb steeply. I run over and see that it's an old man, who must have lost his footing on the icy path and then failed to get up. I help him to his feet, I can still feel the rough cloth of his coat and recollect the naphthalene smell it gives off. The man seems unhurt, but his face is blue with cold, his lips almost white. I ask him where he's come from. He is hard to understand but I guess from his reply that he lives in the old folks' home, a home for single elderly men, a Christian charitable institution. I tell him I will take him back there, but he doesn't want to go back, he points to the other bank of the river, and says something I don't understand. It takes some time before I've persuaded him. When he finally gives in, it's as though he's lost all his strength, and I need to take him under the arms and practically carry him so that he doesn't collapse.

The old men's home isn't far, but it takes us a good half an hour to get there. The old man has pushed his arm through mine, his back is so crooked that it's almost horizontal. All the time, he speaks barely two or three sentences. He seems confused, says something about a woman he went out walking with. As we're walking, it seems to me there's something linking us, something much deeper than language, as though we were a single being, a quadruped, both old and young, half-beginning, half-ending.

The men's home is a big old building standing in a gully off to one side next to a railway viaduct. I have to think of all the biographies that have ended here over the years, all the solitary old men who lived there, waiting to die, nothing more. In summer, they sit outside the building, chew on cheap cigars, walk through the village as though they had some kind of objective. People know who they are, say hello to them even if they don't say hello back, only when one of them dies, no one misses him.

The old man says nothing more. I wish him all the best and watch him as he struggles up the stairs and opens the battered wooden door. I picture him walking up the steps inside with still more difficulty, one step after the other, to the first floor, where his room is. It's cold and grim in the corridors, and smells of coffee and bleach and old people. I picture his small bare room, his few possessions, no more than would fit in a single suitcase. When the old man dies, everything will go in the trash, because he has no next of kin, or no one is interested in his junk, not even a few black-and-white photographs he had of long-since-deceased individuals, his parents or grandparents, distant relatives, maybe a young woman he was once in love with.

And while I go home, I imagine ending up like him, slipping away freed of all obligations, leaving no traces.

Falling down on an icy path, and, unable to get up, eventually giving in. The rhythm of my breathing settles, I no longer feel the cold. I think of my life which hasn't happened yet, fuzzy scenes, dark cutout figures against the light, distant voices. The strange thing is that there was never anything mournful about this fantasy, not even then, it was something to be wished for, it had a clarity and correctness, like this long-ago winter morning itself.

PETER STAMM is the author of the novels *To the Back of Beyond, All Days Are Night, Seven Years, On a Day Like This, Unformed Landscape,* and *Agnes* and the short-story collections *We're Flying* and *In Strange Gardens and Other Stories.* His award-winning books have been translated into more than thirty languages. For his entire body of work and his accomplishments in fiction, he was short-listed for the Man Booker International Prize in 2013, and in 2014 he won the prestigious Friedrich Hölderlin Prize. He lives in Switzerland.

MICHAEL HOFMANN has translated the work of Gottfried Benn, Hans Fallada, Franz Kafka, Joseph Roth, and many others. In 2012 he was awarded the Thornton Wilder Prize for Translation by the American Academy of Arts and Letters. His *Selected Poems* was published in 2009, and *Where Have You Been? Selected Essays* in 2014. He lives in Florida and London.

▛ OTHER PRESS

You might also enjoy these titles from Peter Stamm:

TO THE BACK OF BEYOND

Unfailingly perceptive and precise, this novel gives form to doubts that disturb us all: Are we being true to ourselves? Are we loved for our true selves?

"Exceptionally moving writing." —*The Guardian*

"[A] work about freedom and wanting. Stamm's superb descriptions of alpine nature and internal human conflict are aided by Hofmann's excellent translation." —*Publishers Weekly*

AGNES

In this unforgettable and haunting novel, Stamm incisively examines the power of storytelling to influence thought and behavior, reaching a chilling conclusion.

"A kind of parable . . . simple and haunting."
—*New York Review of Books*

"*Agnes* is a moody, unsettled, and elusive little fable — and it's always interesting." —*Wall Street Journal*

SEVEN YEARS

Torn between his highbrow marriage and his lowbrow affair, Alex is stuck within a spiraling threesome. *Seven Years* is a bold, sobering novel about the quest for love.

"*Seven Years* is a novel to make you doubt your own dogma. What more can a novel do than that?"
—Zadie Smith, *Harper's Magazine*

Also recommended:

ALL DAYS ARE NIGHT

In unadorned and haunting style, this novel forcefully tells the story of a woman who loses her life but must stay alive all the same.

"[A] complex, psychological tale . . . riveting . . . intensely moving." —*Wall Street Journal*

"[An] engrossing story of recovery." —*New Yorker*

"A postmodern riff on *The Magic Mountain* . . . a page-turner." —*The Atlantic*

UNFORMED LANDSCAPE

A sensitive young woman is led to the richer life she was meant to have and is brave enough to claim. Her story speaks eloquently about solitude, the fragility of love, lost illusions, and self-discovery.

"Like the landscapes of his novels, Stamm's prose is spare and graceful." —*New Republic*

WE'RE FLYING

This short-story collection is a superb introduction to the work of Peter Stamm and its precise rendering of the contemporary human psyche.

"The situations depicted in *We're Flying* . . . evoke the negative spaces of Raymond Carver or the quiet menace of Shirley Jackson, but with Walser's light touch." —*Seattle Times*

▓ OTHER PRESS

www.otherpress.com